"Garrick, exactly how long have I been pregnant?"

"About twelve weeks," he admitted.

Samantha shook her head slowly. "You married me because I was pregnant, didn't you?"

"Not exactly."

"Then why?"

"I married you," he said, "because I thought we had a good chance of being happy together." They did. Ten years of friendship was the strongest basis for marriage he could imagine.

"And because you got me pregnant," Samantha said.

"Your pregnancy did have something to do with it," he admitted.

She looked disappointed. "You don't love me?"

If only she knew what she was saying! But he couldn't tell her the truth. Even amnesia wasn't enough to erase the last ten years.

Dear Reader,

The month of June makes me think of June brides, Father's Day and the first bloom of summer love. And Silhouette Romance is celebrating the start of summer with six wonderful books about love and romance.

Our BUNDLE OF JOY this month is delivered by Stella Bagwell's *The Tycoon's Tots*—her thirtieth Silhouette book. As her TWINS ON THE DOORSTEP miniseries continues, we finally discover who gets to keep those adorable babies...*and* find romance in the bargain.

Elizabeth August is back with her much-loved SMYTHESHIRE, MASSACHUSETTS series. In *The Determined Virgin* you'll meet a woman whose marriage of convenience is proving to be very *in*convenient, thanks to her intense attraction to her "in-name-only" husband.

BACHELOR GULCH is a little town that needs women, *and* the name of Sandra Steffen's brand-new miniseries. The fun begins in *Luke's Would-Be Bride* as a local bachelor falls for his feisty receptionist—the one woman in town *not* looking for a husband!

And there are plenty more compelling romances for you this month: A lovely lady rancher can't wait to hightail it out of Texas—till she meets her handsome new foreman in Leanna Wilson's *Lone Star Rancher*. A new husband can't bear to tell his amnesiac bride that the baby she's carrying isn't his, in *Her Forgotten Husband* by Anne Ha. And one lucky cowboy discovers a night of passion has just made him a daddy in Teresa Southwick's *The Bachelor's Baby*.

I hope you enjoy all of June's books!

Melissa Senate,
Senior Editor

Silhouette Romance

Please address questions and book requests to:
Silhouette Reader Service
U.S.: 3010 Walden Ave., P.O. Box 1325, Buffalo, NY 14269
Canadian: P.O. Box 609, Fort Erie, Ont. L2A 5X3

HER FORGOTTEN HUSBAND

Anne Ha

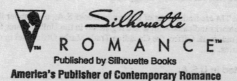

Silhouette

ROMANCE™

Published by Silhouette Books

America's Publisher of Contemporary Romance

For Ben and Patti, with lots of groovy love.

Many thanks to Monica Caltabiano for her fabulous
critiquing, to Rachel Jones for strategically timed
brainstorming and to Donna Jean for those lifesaving
ice-cream breaks.

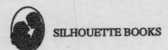 SILHOUETTE BOOKS

ISBN 0-373-19232-0

HER FORGOTTEN HUSBAND

Books by Anne Ha

Silhouette Romance

Husband Next Door #1208
Her Forgotten Husband #1232

ANNE HA

is the pen name of Anne and Joe Thoron, a husband-and-wife writing team. College sweethearts, they live in Oregon with two naughty cats and a vegetable garden. They love to travel and meet all different kinds of people. Their first book, *Husband Next Door*, was a finalist for the Romance Writers of America's Golden Heart Award.

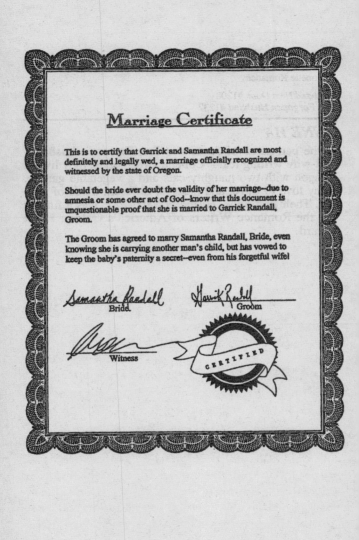

Marriage Certificate

This is to certify that Garrick and Samantha Randall are most definitely and legally wed, a marriage officially recognized and witnessed by the state of Oregon.

Should the bride ever doubt the validity of her marriage--due to amnesia or some other act of God--know that this document is unquestionable proof that she is married to Garrick Randall, Groom.

The Groom has agreed to marry Samantha Randall, Bride, even knowing she is carrying another man's child, but has vowed to keep the baby's paternity a secret--even from his forgetful wife!

Samantha Randall
Bride

Garrick Randall
Groom

[signature]
Witness

CERTIFIED

Chapter One

He seemed quite sane.

The handsome man seated by her bed—the man cradling her hand in his and murmuring endearments—did not appear demented, deranged or otherwise unbalanced.

But she'd never seen him before in her life.

He was a total stranger.

A moment ago she'd awakened, blinking in the bright hospital lights, to his inexplicable presence. She hated to spoil his pleasure, his obvious relief, but she couldn't go on acting as if she knew him.

Gently she pulled her hand from his grasp and edged a few inches away.

"Sweetheart?" The man's voice was deep and husky. A few days' beard growth shadowed his jaw, giving him a sensual, tousled look which grew more pronounced as he raked his fingers through his dark brown hair. "You're not still angry?"

Angry? Now there was a question that didn't make sense! She had no reason to be angry. The only thing bothering her was the pounding ache in her head. It grew worse with every passing second.

Raising a hand to massage her temple, she drew back when her fingers encountered soft gauze. A bandage! Amazed, she gingerly traced the gauze, wincing at a shaft of pain.

"You all right?" the stranger asked.

"My head hurts," she said, and shut her eyes. The darkness brought relief, wrapping her in its safe cocoon.

"I'm sure it does, after the wallop you gave it. You've had a concussion, you know."

She frowned, eyes still closed. "I have?"

"Two days ago. Your car went off that nasty curve on Humphrey Boulevard. It hit a tree, but you were lucky—just suffered the concussion and a few cuts and bruises."

She couldn't bring herself to reply. It was easier to lie still between the starched white hospital sheets, to let the blankness ease the pain.

Briefly the stranger touched her shoulder, his fingers warming her skin. It felt nice, she thought, a bit guiltily. She heard him move, knew he stood over the bed. Heat emanated from his body, and she breathed in the spicy male scent of him. It wasn't at all familiar, but it was oddly compelling.

"I'll tell the doctor you're awake," he said.

But he didn't leave, and she had the feeling he watched her intently.

After a moment he kissed her forehead, the contact light and fleeting. "I'm glad you're all right, Sam. If I'd lost you..."

She opened her eyes, caught by one word. "Sam?"

He straightened, giving her a tired smile. "Sorry. I meant to say Samantha. I'll get used to it someday."

"Samantha," she echoed. Confusion and anxiety rose inside her. Who in the world was Samantha?

Not her, surely. She didn't feel like a Samantha. She felt like a...like a...

Nothing came to mind. No name seemed to fit.

Meeting the stranger's expectant gaze, she struggled not to show her distress. She opened her mouth, but couldn't speak. She felt lost, adrift.

Closing her eyes again, she tried to make sense of her situation. She knew she lay in a hospital room, could recognize its antiseptic smells. She knew the prickling discomfort in her left arm was caused by an IV needle, that the humming sound came from fluorescent lights.

But that was where it stopped. She didn't know who she was. Or where she lived or how old she was or what kind of car she drove.

Oh, good Lord, she thought. She didn't even know if she had any family or what she did for a living...

The man cleared his throat, interrupting her panic attack. "By the way," he said, his voice soft. "The baby is fine."

At first she thought she hadn't heard him correctly.

She swallowed and stared up at him, unable to keep the bewilderment from her face. "The, uh, baby?"

Could she be a *mother*? It didn't seem possible. She had absolutely no recollection of changing diapers or of getting up for nighttime feedings. No recollection of childbirth.

"Yes," the stranger answered. "The doctor said the accident had no ill effects."

She grimaced, still not sure she had a baby. But maybe she would remember him—or was it her?—and would feel overjoyed it hadn't been hurt. In the meantime all she could do was smile and try to think of something to say.

"Thank goodness for car seats!" she managed.

The man didn't smile back. In fact, he looked decidedly concerned. His brows lowered and his slate gray eyes narrowed.

Darn it. Obviously she hadn't been maternal enough. She tried again. "Thanks for the reassurance. I feel so much better knowing my baby is okay. I'm really looking forward to holding...it...in my arms again."

His frown deepened. "Samantha..."

What did he want from her? So what if she couldn't remember the gender of her child? A few seconds ago she hadn't even known she had a baby, and now he was trying to hold her to some unreachable maternal ideal.

"Are you sure you're okay?"

"I'm fine," she snapped.

He sat back down on the chair, holding her hand

while he studied her face. She felt as if he were trying to gaze into her soul. And he didn't seem pleased by what he saw.

"Samantha," he said, "there's something you should know." He paused, appearing to choose his words with care. "The baby wasn't in a car seat."

"What?" she blurted. He was lying. He had to be. She couldn't have been so irresponsible! "Look, mister, I don't know what bee flew into your bonnet today, but I do *not* appreciate your accusations of neglect. Of course I put my child in a car seat!"

He shook his head slowly, those watchful gray eyes still on her.

"And before you make any more snide comments on my parenting," she added, "go out and try it yourself. It's not as easy as it looks."

In response to her bravado, an annoying grin tugged at the corners of his mouth—his very attractive, sensuous mouth.

She scowled, unable to see what he found so amusing.

"Samantha," he said, "the baby wasn't in a car seat because it hasn't been born yet."

She was so relieved she hadn't been a neglectful mother that the full import of his words didn't immediately sink in.

When it did, she glanced down at her stomach, then slowly reached out to feel it. Through the sheet, she cupped her hand around the slight curve of her abdomen. Was that a baby? Or just her body's normal shape? She had no way of knowing.

"I'm pregnant?" she asked. She didn't *feel* particularly pregnant.

He nodded.

"Are you sure?"

"Very."

Her gaze returned to her belly. He sounded adamant. Too adamant not to be right.

She felt a sudden wave of tenderness, thinking a new life grew within her. She was fiercely glad her baby hadn't been harmed in the crash. "I haven't been this way for long, have I?"

"No, not that long."

She couldn't take her eyes off her stomach. A baby! How wonderful and strange.

Then an awkward thought occurred to her. She didn't know how to ask at first, but then realized she didn't need to ask at all. Instead, she looked down at the fingers of her left hand. Yes, she wore a wedding ring.

The stranger followed her gaze. "I slipped it back on this morning," he said, as if it was a confession.

She peered at the simple gold band. "I'm married." Her voice was full of wonder.

Still holding her other hand, he gave it a squeeze. "It certainly appears that way."

The band was delicate and nicely proportioned, she noted, but it wasn't in any way familiar. It didn't spark any memories. "I'm married," she said again.

"Yes."

She sighed. "That's a relief. I don't think I'd like

to be a single mother.... You wouldn't, er, happen to know who my husband is, would you?''

''As a matter of fact, I would.''

''Who is it?''

His expression turned wry. He raised her fingers to his mouth, kissed them with warm, gentle lips and said, ''Me.''

She snatched her hand from his grasp. ''You?''

The man nodded. ''Yes, me.''

She stared at him, not wanting to believe she could be married to a man she didn't even recognize. ''That's—that's crazy. I didn't marry you. You don't know what you're talking about. I've never seen you before in my life.''

He shook his head. ''It's definitely time to get the doctor.''

''But—''

''I'll be right back,'' he told her, and left.

She blew out a stream of air. ''I would never,'' she said to the empty room, ''marry such an impossible man.''

True, he *was* attractive. Extremely attractive. His body was long and lean, and his sculpted features made him look like a Greek god. Maybe she'd been carried away on a tide of desire.

No, no, she couldn't be married to him. She couldn't have kissed a man like him, have lain in his arms, and not remembered it. Somehow she knew the power of his lovemaking would sear into her soul. She'd have remembered it.

The power of his lovemaking...

Good grief! She'd only known the man ten minutes, and already she was mentally having her way with him. It wasn't like her to fantasize about strangers. She'd always reserved her fantasies for...for...

The wisp of memory, if that was what it was, slipped from her grasp like a ribbon of smoke. She closed her eyes as her headache intensified.

What was the name? She'd been about to think of a man's name.

But it didn't come, and the more she struggled to retrieve it, the more her head pounded.

Anyway, she told herself, what was the point of remembering some guy's name, when she didn't even know her own?

The stranger, of course, had called her Samantha. Could that really be right? She said it out loud a few times, trying to accustom herself. It sounded foreign to her own ears, as did her voice.

She started when the door to her room swung open. The stranger walked back in, accompanied by two women. She wasn't ready for them yet, she thought. She wanted more time to orient herself, to get control of the situation.

One of the women, dressed in a doctor's coat, approached her. She studied the machines above the bed, then held up a light and briefly shone it into each of her eyes. "I'm Dr. Hernandez," she said in a friendly, soothing tone. "How are you feeling?"

"Fine. Except for this awful headache."

Dr. Hernandez nodded. The other woman, who appeared to be a nurse, handed her a chart on a clipboard. The doctor made a few notations. "That's normal in a case such as this. Can you tell me your name?"

She debated for a moment. Technically the answer was no. But if she gave them the name the man had called her, maybe they'd leave her alone. "Samantha," she said brightly.

The others exchanged glances.

"Samantha what?" Dr. Hernandez asked.

She stared meditatively up at the ceiling. "Samantha...er...Bergman?"

Silence.

"Samantha Bogart?"

Silence.

"Hepburn? Tracy?" She wasn't getting anywhere. And the man looked amused again. She glared at him. "All right, so I don't know my last name. So what does that prove?"

The doctor patted her arm and continued the examination. "It appears you've suffered some memory loss. Do you know what city you're in?"

She searched her mind for the name of a city. "Um, New York?"

Dr. Hernandez shook her head. "Sorry. You're in Portland, Oregon. According to your husband, you've lived here all your life." She glanced at the man beside her. "Garrick tells me you don't believe you're married to him."

"I'm not." It sounded petulant, but she didn't care. She felt exposed and vulnerable, as if she were the butt of a joke that everyone got but her. She narrowed her eyes on her so-called husband. "Garrick?" she said. "Is that your name?"

He nodded.

"But I've never heard it before in my life. First name or last?"

"First. It's Garrick Randall."

The doctor patted her arm again. "I know this must be a confusing time for you, but he is your husband. The hospital verified it. Now, I expect to release you into his care tomorrow, after we run a few more tests. As long as you're recovering well from the blow to your head, and it hasn't hurt your pregnancy, there's no reason to keep you here."

"But what about my memory? Shouldn't I stay until I get it back?" She felt intense trepidation at the idea of leaving the hospital, leaving the only world she'd known so far. Especially if she had to leave with a man she couldn't remember.

Dr. Hernandez pursed her lips. "Unfortunately, Samantha, there's nothing we can do about your memory. It may return in a few hours or a few days, or it may drift slowly back over a period of months." She smiled gently. "I'll have a counselor speak with you about it first thing tomorrow."

A few minutes later the doctor left with Garrick. The nurse removed the IV, smoothed the covers and turned off the overhead lights before following them.

Then she was alone. It wasn't as much of a relief as she'd thought it would be. In the light from the single fixture by the bed, the room seemed unbearably stark. There was one small window, but it revealed only darkness and a few distant street lamps. She wondered how many hours she would have to endure before morning.

She closed her eyes and tried to sleep, but she'd been fast asleep for two whole days, so she knew it was futile.

Garrick kept slipping into her mind, with his tousled dark hair and appealing male scent. She almost missed him.

Well, she supposed that made sense. It really did seem as if she'd married him. And she'd probably done it for a good reason. She probably loved him!

Too bad she couldn't remember.

She still didn't feel like a Samantha, she thought. Maybe she never would. Maybe she'd always hated the name.

The door swung open with a quiet swish, and Garrick entered. He met her eyes and smiled a tender, disturbingly sexy smile.

"I thought you'd gone home," she said.

"Eager to be rid of me?"

Mutely she shook her head. On the contrary, his presence gave her pleasure—but she wasn't quite willing to admit it.

He crossed to the chair and picked up an overnight bag that had been stashed beneath it. His back to her, he rummaged through the contents.

Samantha watched him while he did so. He wore faded jeans and a wrinkled white oxford shirt that emphasized the breadth of his shoulders. She could see his muscles shift underneath it as he moved.

This man was her husband, she thought. The father of the small life growing inside her. How...odd.

Even though she couldn't remember it, she'd actually made love with him. She'd run her fingers over his warm skin, kissed his full, sensuous lips.

And other places as well.

Despite the pounding in her head, a spark of excitement ran through her. There must be worse fates than being married to such an attractive man, she decided. Even if he was a little maddening.

He turned to face her. His features had a rugged beauty that drew her gaze to his beard-darkened cheeks and the line of his jaw. His gray eyes were like sun-warmed granite—hard but not cold.

Samantha's attention drifted downward. Garrick wore his sleeves rolled back, revealing muscled forearms lightly sprinkled with hair. His legs were strong and well shaped, his hips lean. He had the body of a man who enjoyed physical activity, who skied, played tennis, jogged, made love....

She felt a sudden urge to touch him, to learn with her fingertips whether his body was as strong and firm as it looked.

Garrick's hands came up and unfastened the top button of his shirt. She watched, mesmerized, as deft fingers slid the second button free. And the third. She saw dark hair curling on the sharply defined planes of his chest.

Her mouth went dry.

Three more buttons. He tugged the shirt free of his waistband, revealing a washboard stomach.

"What are you doing?" she croaked.

His hands stilled, but he didn't answer. The shirt hung loose around his torso. Dark hair arrowed down his stomach and disappeared under his waistband.

She swallowed painfully.

With blessedly quick movements, Garrick shed the wrinkled oxford and replaced it with a black T-shirt.

Samantha cursed herself for a fool. She'd acted as if he were putting on some sort of striptease, as if he could read her mind and the unseemly thoughts that went on in it, when he'd only been changing.

They were married, she reminded herself. There was no reason for him not to change his shirt in front of her—especially when it looked as if he'd slept in it for a week.

He handed her a square leather purse. "I thought you might want this."

Happy for a distraction, Samantha took the purse. She sorted through its contents, hoping something would look familiar.

Nothing did. The pocket calendar, face powder, lipstick and address book might all have belonged to someone else. Even her driver's license, which showed a five-foot-five, twenty-five-year-old woman with brown eyes and long blond hair, didn't elicit a flicker of recognition. She flipped through the address book without knowing a single one of the names that were written in a slanted, flowing script. Sighing, she put everything back in the purse.

"Nothing?" he asked.

"Not a thing. It's like digging into someone else's purse. I feel like a trespasser." She held out the driver's license. "Do I really look like this?"

He glanced at the license, then at her. "Close enough, though it's not the most flattering picture—makes your hair look limp and your eyes look small and beady."

"Thanks."

He grinned back at her. "You asked."

Samantha fingered a lock of her hair, which was loosely tied at the nape of her neck. The strands felt thick and soft. She pulled it over her shoulder to inspect it, but the unfamiliarity of the pale gold color disturbed her.

"There's a mirror in the bathroom, in case you'd like to see your face."

Something made her shake her head, despite her curiosity. The throbbing headache grew sharper with her movement.

She told herself it would be too much trouble to get out of bed, but in the back of her mind she knew her response was more complicated. If she looked in the mirror, she would have to confront a stranger's face—even though she'd had it for twenty-five years. She wasn't sure if she was ready for such a highly charged encounter.

The magnitude of her situation finally struck her full force. She knew nothing at all about herself or her life. She had only what she could learn from the foreign-looking items in her purse, and from Garrick. Without them she'd be completely at a loss.

It made her feel vulnerable, helpless.

It made her feel like a nonentity.

Garrick watched the expressions play across Samantha's face. She'd never been good at hiding her thoughts and emotions. He could tell her panic had returned.

Taking her hand, he held it once more between his. "It'll be okay, Sam. Your memory will return."

She stared back at him, her brown eyes dazed. "When?"

Garrick paused. He still had trouble comprehending the fact that she'd lost her memory. How could her whole life disappear just like that? How could she not remember the past ten years? It must be utterly overwhelming. "I don't know, Sam," he said. "But I'll stay with you and support you till it does."

She lay back. "I'm scared."

"I know you are. Everything will be all right, though. You and the baby are alive, and that's what matters." He stroked her hand until she slowly relaxed. Amazing, he thought, that his touch could have such an effect on her, as if she drew strength from him, from his nearness.

Garrick had had the same feeling when she'd been unconscious, as if he was speeding her recovery merely by touching her and remaining by her side. She'd become skittish and uncertain once she'd woken, but now the connection was back, and thank goodness. It gave him hope for the future.

Garrick found himself wishing her memory would take a while to return. He knew it was a foolish, selfish thought, but he couldn't stop it. He wanted the chance to build a new intimacy between them, to make their marriage a strong and fulfilling one—and not just a passionless arrangement.

Samantha squeezed his hand. "Who am I, Garrick? Where do I live? What do I do?" She smiled ruefully. "Why am I such a bad driver?"

He laughed softly. She had a lot of courage, he thought, to make a joke—even a feeble one—when her life was in chaos. "You're not a bad driver," he assured her.

"I hit a tree. You told me so yourself. How much worse could I be?"

Garrick looked down at her, wishing he knew how to reply. He could have told her she'd been distraught, that her mental state had destroyed her concentration. But he didn't. If he told her everything about her accident, about the convoluted events that had led up to it, they'd be right back where they'd been two days ago.

"Well?" she said. "Aren't you going to tell me anything?"

He studied her for a long moment. "You're definitely not a bad driver. What else would you like to know?"

"How long ago did we meet?"

"Ten years."

She considered this. "So it wasn't a whirlwind courtship."

"No." It wasn't a courtship at all, really, but she didn't need to know that right now.

"How long have we been married?"

Garrick groaned inwardly. These probably seemed like simple questions to her, but they were headed in a difficult direction. "Two months," he admitted.

She was clearly shocked. "That's all? We certainly took our own sweet time, didn't we? Why the delay?"

"You were only fifteen when I met you," he pointed out, unable to keep from smiling. She had no way of knowing how attracted he'd been, even back then.

"And how old were you?"

"Twenty."

"Ah..." she said, a look of dawning comprehension on her face. "Let me see. I must have fallen in love with you on the spot. I can just picture it—the shy girl and the handsome older man. How sweet." She paused, her brown eyes wistful. "Was I shy?"

"Yes, you were shy." He remembered their first meeting as clearly as if it were yesterday. He and Warren had both come home from college for the winter holidays. Their younger sister Jenny had rushed down the stairs to greet them, eager to introduce her new friend. Samantha had followed with tentative steps.

Garrick had heard all about Samantha in Jenny's letters and been prepared to like her. He had not been prepared, however, for the jolt of desire that swept through him at the sight of her blossoming figure and ethereal brown eyes. She was fifteen, he'd reminded himself sharply. A *child.*

Someday, he'd thought as he'd pushed back his desire, she would be grown up, a woman far more beautiful than the child in front of him. He would wait, and the waiting would make it all the more pleasurable in the end.

But looking into her eyes and seeing the barely concealed hero worship in them had been difficult indeed.

"You must have been amused by my crush," she said.

"Not at all," he responded truthfully.

"Of course not." She smiled. "You probably didn't notice I was madly in love with you. I was fifteen, you said? You probably didn't even know I was alive."

Of course he'd known. But Garrick didn't relish reliving that part of the past any more than necessary. "Anything else you'd like me to tell you?" he asked, hoping to shift the conversation to safer topics.

She thought for a moment, tapping her chin in that adorable way she had. "Where'd we go on our honeymoon? Maybe it will help me remember."

He hesitated. "We stayed here in town."

"Really? No trip to Hawaii or Mexico? Was that my choice or yours?"

"Both of ours."

Samantha frowned. "Isn't this strange? I can remember about Hawaii and Mexico, but I don't know if I've been to either one or if I learned about them from TV."

"You've been to Mexico, not Hawaii," Garrick said.

"With you?"

"With Jenny."

"Who's Jenny?"

"Your best friend. My sister."

"Oh." She looked a little depressed. "I can't believe I don't remember my own best friend."

"It's okay, Sam. I'm sure she'll understand. She'd be here right now, by the way, but she's taking an exam."

Samantha gave him a questioning look.

"Law school," he explained. "She's finishing her second year." He decided he'd given Samantha enough information to absorb for one night. "How's your headache?"

She closed her eyes briefly. "Better, but the medication they gave me isn't very strong. I guess they didn't want to hurt the baby." As if suddenly reminded of the new life growing inside her, she cupped a hand to her abdomen. She grinned at him, her eyes alight. "We sure got started on our family fast, didn't we?"

Garrick grimaced. Now what the hell was he supposed to say to that?

Chapter Two

He racked his brains for the right response.

It didn't come.

If he told Samantha the truth about the baby's conception... Well, he didn't know how she'd react. But after her romanticized version of their relationship, she was sure to be upset.

Samantha continued, unaware of his inner turmoil. "After ten years of being madly in love with you, I couldn't wait to start a family, right? Or was it just because you're, er, extremely virile...? No point going to Hawaii if you're gonna spend the whole week inside the hotel room, anyway, eh?"

"I guess not," he said, feeling trapped. He was pretty damn close to lying by omission at this point.

He should just tell her everything. That was the honorable thing to do. But when he opened his mouth, no words came out. He just stared at her beautiful features, which were so much more happy and relaxed than they'd been twenty minutes ago, and couldn't bring himself to burst her bubble.

"Two months," Samantha continued in wonderment. "I bet I never thought I'd get pregnant that quickly. Did you?"

"Uh, not exactly."

She paused, tapping her chin. "Is that why we fought?"

"Why we fought?" he repeated.

"Yes. When I woke up, you asked if I was still angry. So we must have had a fight, right? Was it about the baby?"

Garrick nodded reluctantly. She might have lost her memory, but her instincts were right on. They *had* been fighting about the baby right before she drove off. But it wasn't what she thought.

Samantha's brows drew together. "You don't want the baby, do you?" She shut her eyes. "Oh, gosh, no wonder I got amnesia. I don't want to remember that you don't want our baby!"

"Sam," he said, leaning forward, "I want this baby, and I have since the moment you told me you were pregnant. Nothing could make me give it up." And it was the truth. Despite everything, he already loved the child she carried.

"Then why were we fighting?"

He sighed. "I can't explain that right now. I don't even understand it myself. It was all a big mistake, which you'll realize when you're better."

"You want the baby?"

"Yes, I want the baby."

Samantha sank back against the cushions, an expression of relief on her face. She folded her hands over her belly. "The doctor said it's May," she mused. "So am I going to give birth in December?"

Oh, good Lord. She'd always been too mathematical. "November, actually."

Her eyes widened. "November?"

"Early November," he said, feeling as if he'd just stepped off the edge of a precipice.

She stared at him. "Garrick, exactly how long have I been pregnant?"

"About twelve weeks," he admitted.

"Oh... Oh, no." She shook her head slowly. "You married me because I got pregnant, didn't you?"

How could something be true and yet so completely false? He remembered how quickly his shock at her pregnancy had shifted to elation—and how he'd hated himself for that weakness. He'd had to force himself not to blurt his proposal on the spot, but to pull back behind a screen of disinterest, treating the situation as he might treat a sensitive business deal. "Not exactly."

"Then why?"

"I married you," he said, "because I thought we had a good chance of being happy together."

They did. Ten years of friendship was the strongest basis for marriage he could imagine.

"And because you got me pregnant," Samantha said.

"Your pregnancy did have something to do with it," he admitted.

She looked disappointed. "You don't love me?"

If she only knew what she was saying! But he couldn't tell her the truth. Even amnesia wasn't enough to erase the past ten years.

Garrick kept the emotion from his voice, just as he'd done when he'd proposed. "Love isn't always the most important thing, Sam... Sometimes friendship can be enough."

He didn't love her.

Sure, he'd married her and wanted their baby, but he didn't love her. He'd spent the whole night by her side, but he didn't love her.

It wasn't right, Samantha thought the next morning as Garrick checked her out of the hospital. Something felt wrong. She might not remember who she was, but she knew, just knew, she wouldn't have wanted a loveless marriage.

So why had she married him? Only because she was pregnant? That didn't make sense. She wouldn't have slept with him unless...

She loved him. *She* loved *him*. Obviously the adolescent love she'd imagined last night had been all too real.

But he hadn't loved her back.

Had she known? Had she willingly settled for a one-way marriage in order to be with her childhood crush? Or had she thought their feelings were mutual? Maybe she'd found out he didn't love her, and that was what they'd fought about, what had made her such a terrible driver the night of her accident.

Maybe he'd let her think he loved her to get her to have a fling, but then it had backfired when she'd gotten pregnant.

She considered Garrick as he helped her into his dark green sedan, his touch warm and reassuring on her arm. He radiated confidence, strength and purpose. He didn't seem like the devious type, she thought, the type to take advantage of a young girl's crush.

Which left a distressing alternative. Maybe she'd taken advantage of him.

Samantha watched Garrick circle to the driver's side, his dark hair lifting in the wind. Today he wore a blue chambray shirt and casual khaki chinos. He looked every bit as sexy as he had last night, and again she felt the pull of attraction and desire. He was an incredibly handsome man.

Could she have done it?

She didn't want to face the possibility, but she couldn't ignore it: she was pregnant, and he'd admitted that had something to do with their marriage. So had she set out to seduce him? Had she planned to get pregnant to entrap him?

If she had, she wasn't at all sure she wanted to regain her memory.

Garrick pulled out of the hospital complex and joined the flow of traffic down the hill. "Feeling okay?" he asked her. "Does it upset you to be in a car?"

Samantha shook her head, unable to voice her troubled thoughts. Deliberately she smiled and relaxed her grip on her purse. "I'm fine," she said. "The car doesn't bother me at all."

It was true, too. Garrick's car felt comfortable, solid and sturdy, and he drove with competent ease. She wondered how many times she'd ridden in it with him.

Reaching the bottom of the hill, they drove along a few city streets and then uphill again on a steep, curvy road. The trees arching over the roadway were thick with spring leaves, and warm air swept in through the open window. They passed large houses set back from the road.

Nothing was familiar.

"Have I been on this road before?"

He glanced over at her. "It's the quickest route from your old apartment to the house. You probably drove it when you came to visit Jenny."

"Oh. Where was my apartment?"

"Across the river, about fifteen minutes from here."

"Did I live there until we got married?"

He nodded. "We can go see it sometime, if you'd like. Maybe it will spark a memory."

And maybe it wouldn't. Maybe her previous life would always remain a total blank, the good memories gone along with the bad.

She wondered suddenly where they'd made love that first time, when she'd seduced him. Had she lured him back to her apartment under false pretenses, or had she brazenly invited herself into his bed? Maybe she'd attacked him at his office, or in a dumpy motel room. She wondered whether she had good memories of that hour in his arms, or bad.

Looking at Garrick's virile male form on the leather seat beside her, at his capable hands on the steering wheel, Samantha was pretty sure the memories were good. At least the ones of their lovemaking.

"Samantha?"

She flushed. "Sorry," she said. "I was just thinking. We can go by the apartment tomorrow if you think it would help."

"Why don't we see how you're feeling? You may need a few days' rest."

Rest wasn't high on Samantha's list of priorities, even though she knew her body needed it. She didn't want to spend long hours alone in a house she didn't remember, surrounded by possessions that didn't rekindle any of her lost memories. She couldn't imagine anything more lonely.

It would be better to get a good night's sleep and go to work in the morning, even though Dr. Hernandez had said she shouldn't.

She caught herself. How could she go to work? She didn't know where she worked, much less what she did. And how would she remember what to do? For that matter, she couldn't even be sure she was employed!

"Do I have a job?" she asked.

"Yes."

"What do I do?"

"You're the assistant marketing director of an office supply firm."

"Oh." Samantha took a moment to digest this. What did such a position entail? It sounded strange and intimidating, as if she were hearing about someone else's job rather than her own.

She took stock of her clothes—a pair of wheat-colored jeans and a plain white T-shirt, which Garrick had brought her that morning. It didn't look like the sort of outfit an assistant marketing director would wear.

"Are you sure I don't deliver pizzas or rent out movies at the video store?"

He smiled. "No, you're definitely in marketing, and you're very good at your job."

"I don't remember anything about it."

"You will," he replied. "In any case, they've got you covered. You'd planned an extended maternity leave, and they'd already started to prepare for your absence. This is a little sooner than expected, of course, but there's no rush to get back before your memory returns."

"If it ever does," she muttered.

Garrick took a hand from the steering wheel and placed it on her knee. The gesture was meant to comfort, she knew, but its effect was less than soothing. The warmth of him burned through the fabric of her jeans, shooting sparks of awareness up her body.

Disturbed she could be so affected by a man she knew didn't love her, Samantha wanted to pull away.

Garrick spared her the effort. He lifted his hand quickly, frowning as if he, too, was bothered by the casual contact.

"Don't worry," he said after a moment. "Whatever happens, you'll be able to deal with it. You've always been levelheaded, Samantha."

For some reason this disappointed her. The way he said it made her sound almost boring. "Always?"

He studied her for a long moment. "No, not always... I wouldn't have married you if you didn't have an adventurous streak."

Garrick's meaning was clear enough. He might as well have said straight out that he'd only married her because she'd gotten pregnant. The only surprising thing was that his voice wasn't bitter. It was almost as if he didn't mind being trapped into marrying her.

She must have misinterpreted his tone, she decided. Perhaps her concussion had affected her perception. Or perhaps it was the effects of carrying the baby.

The baby. Samantha gazed down at her abdomen.

Garrick had said he wanted the baby, and she believed him. But would he love her or him, even though he didn't love Samantha? A child needed a lot of attention and nurturing, and if Garrick acted simply out of a sense of duty, surely the child would know. And worse, if he treated his offspring as some sort of unwelcome houseguest, a burden that had been thrust on him by a conniving mother, she wouldn't be able to stand it.

"So," she said, eager to distract herself from her

unpleasant thoughts, "I'm in marketing. What do you do?"

"I'm the president of an office supply firm."

She looked over at him. "The same firm?"

Garrick nodded. "The same firm." He turned the car off the road and drove through a wrought iron gate that stood between two stone pillars flanked by a tall, dense hedge. "We're here," he announced.

They swept down a long drive, rounded a curve, and then the house came into sight.

Samantha swallowed. The house was huge—far larger than any of the ones they'd passed on the way up. Its style looked Georgian, she thought—not knowing how she could remember architecture when she didn't even know her own name—with alternating dark and light red bricks and a massive portico entrance framed by imposing columns. The lawn in front of the house was landscaped with clipped hedges and lush beds of flowers, and a low balustrade bordered the walk.

Samantha clutched her purse full of items she didn't recognize. Even without her memory she knew the house in front of her belonged to a very wealthy family.

And she knew, with the same awful certainty, that she hadn't trapped Garrick Randall into marriage because she'd loved him.

She'd done it for the money.

Hearing the low purr of her brother's car in the driveway, Jenny Randall surveyed her handiwork before leaving Samantha's bedroom.

Everything was ready.

The photo of Samantha and Garrick looked right at home on the nightstand. Samantha was a pretty sixteen, Garrick a debonair twenty-one. His arm lay draped across her shoulder and his expression was playful. Samantha was smiling for the photographer. To someone who didn't know better, it was a sweet picture that hinted at deeper feelings on the part of both people.

And Samantha *didn't* know better—not anymore.

There was a similar photo on Garrick's nightstand, taken a few years later. Jenny had dug both pictures out of her album the night before, after Garrick had called and told her about Samantha's amnesia.

Amnesia—what a stroke of luck!

Jenny glanced at the drawer, which now held a half-empty bottle of scented massage oil. She'd poured out the other half to make it look well used, to give an impression of ongoing eroticism.

She grinned to herself.

Best of all was the lingerie. Samantha's dresser now overflowed with silk and lace creations—washed once to take away the new look—instead of the sturdy cotton undies Samantha had favored before her accident. Jenny had also packed a wickedly tempting bra and panty set with the clothes she'd sent to the hospital with Garrick that morning, so the conversion would be complete.

Many of the items would have to be put aside as

the baby grew, but Jenny had bought several filmy, flowing chemises and nightgowns that would continue to fit. Samantha would look sexy and desirable all the way through her pregnancy, if Jenny had any say in the matter.

She glanced around the room one more time to see if she'd missed anything. Yes, the connecting door. She crossed the room and unlatched the door leading to Garrick's room, propping it open with a heavy doorstop.

It wasn't fair of her to do this, of course. But the doctor had said Samantha's memory might not return for weeks or months—plenty of time for a whole new set of memories to be formed.

And they would. Garrick and Samantha were married now, and Jenny intended them to stay that way. The baby and their wedding were the only good things to come out of the past few months, which had been so difficult for everyone. It was time for some healing, for some much-deserved happiness.

Satisfied with her efforts, Jenny headed downstairs to greet her best friend.

Samantha sat in Garrick's car, frozen, staring up at the huge house. Her stomach felt knotted and tense. "I live *here*?"

"We both do," Garrick said. "Along with Jenny and Beth—that's our mother—and Hugh." He got out of the car and opened her door.

"Who's Hugh? Your father?"

Shaking his head, Garrick helped her up the walkway to the front steps. "Dad died several years ago. Hugh is the, er, housekeeper—for lack of a better word. He hates to be called the butler."

"I see.... So we all live here together? Like on *Dynasty* or something?"

Garrick smiled. "We don't get in each other's way much. It's a good-size house."

Which was exactly what bothered her. "I noticed," she murmured, grimacing.

"Here's Hugh at the door."

Samantha looked up to see the strangest housekeeper imaginable. At least seven feet tall and two hundred and fifty pounds, the man at the top of the steps wore a T-shirt, black jeans and square-toed motorcycle boots. His salt-and-pepper hair was tied back with a leather thong, and he looked as if he ate small children for breakfast.

Her hands strayed protectively to her abdomen.

Hugh's eyes caught the movement. "Morning sickness? Should I make a pot of tea?" His gruff, Hell's Angels voice was all concerned solicitude.

Samantha glanced at Garrick.

He chuckled, as if amused by her trepidation. "He won't bite, Sam."

She felt embarrassed. "Thank you, Hugh, but I'm fine. I haven't had any morning sickness at all." Even last night's headache had subsided.

"Sorry, Hugh." Garrick turned to Samantha. "He wants to try a ginger tea recipe he found in one of our baby books, but you haven't been ill yet—much to his disappointment."

The big, mean-looking housekeeper clucked his tongue as he ushered them inside. "Don't you believe him, Samantha. I'm much happier to have you in perfect health. Welcome home, by the way."

"Thank you," she said, smiling. "Pregnancy does seem to agree with me. I guess it runs in the family, because my mother didn't get sick when she had me, either—" She stopped, surprised.

Hugh's craggy features softened. "Your memory's already returning, I see."

Garrick looked oddly uncomfortable, but said in a calm enough voice, "How much do you remember?"

"I'm not sure. I think I saw her face for a moment. Her skin was soft and...and she used to wear combs in her hair...." Samantha closed her eyes, grasping at the images, but they'd scattered like dust motes blown from a windowsill. "That's all. Except—she's passed away, hasn't she?"

Gently Garrick nodded. "Both of your parents."

Samantha felt a strange sadness knowing she'd never see them again, knowing they'd never meet their grandchild—strange because, though she felt the emotions, she still couldn't remember them.

Hugh gave her a look of sympathy.

At that moment footsteps sounded from above, and they all turned their heads toward the sweeping staircase.

"Samantha? Is that you?" A tall, attractive brunette descended the steps, her blue eyes sparkling. "You're home!"

Samantha blinked. Something about the moment

seemed familiar, though she couldn't put her finger
on it. It certainly wasn't the sight of the young woman's face, which she recognized no more than Garrick's or Hugh's. "Are you Jenny?" she asked.

"Of course I'm Jenny!" The woman rushed across
the entrance hall, her leather flats clacking on the pol-
ished white marble. She enveloped Samantha in a
warm hug. "But you probably can't remember, can
you? Amnesia—how exciting! Oh, Samantha, I'm so
glad you're all right. We were terribly worried, you
know. And Garrick's practically *lived* at the hospital
since your accident...."

She continued in this vein for several minutes, taking Samantha by the arm and leading her back
through the elegant house to an airy breakfast room
filled with potted ferns. The men trailed behind.

Jenny, Samantha and Garrick all sat at the table,
while Hugh disappeared briefly and returned with tall
glasses of iced tea and a cup of milk for Samantha.
He picked up a spray bottle and misted the ferns,
frond by frond, looking incongruous as he handled
the delicate plants.

"Tell me," Jenny said. "When you woke up in the
hospital, what was your first thought?"

Samantha glanced at Garrick. "Well, I guess I
wanted to know who the strange man by my bed
was."

Jenny clapped her hands together, looking tickled.
"You must have been pretty shocked when he told
you he was your husband."

She nodded.

"I bet you were also thrilled, though—I mean, not every girl's lucky enough to have such a hunk for a husband. Oh, this is so romantic! Now you can fall in love with each other all over again!"

"Jenny." Garrick's voice had a tense edge to it. "Let's not overwhelm her."

"I'm not overwhelming her, Garrick. I'm just welcoming her home." She grinned impishly at her brother. "Can I help it if I'm excited for the two of you?"

Garrick shot her a quelling look, but didn't say anything.

Samantha felt she was missing an important part of the conversation, but was too busy trying to interpret Jenny's words to worry about it. Did Jenny really think she and Garrick had been in love? Well, she seemed to have a generally positive outlook on life, so maybe she'd only seen what she'd wanted to see. And hadn't realized love wasn't a factor in the marriage.

Jenny waved a hand around the breakfast room. "Do you really not remember any of this?"

"Nothing," she said.

"She has amnesia," Garrick reminded her.

"I know that," Jenny said. "I know she doesn't remember who we are, or even how much she loves you. And goodness knows she won't remember *that* if you keep being so grouchy. But I've never met an amnesiac before and I want to know what it's like. Do you remember the first day you met Garrick?"

Samantha shook her head.

Jenny leaned forward, her blue eyes alight. "How about the first time he kissed you?"

"Enough, Jenny," Garrick interrupted. "I think we should give Samantha a chance to get her bearings and adjust herself to the fact that she has a family."

Jenny stood up, scowling good-naturedly at him. "Oh, all right." She put a hand on Samantha's shoulder. "Come on, Sam, I'll give you a tour and show you to your room."

Garrick stood, too, looking every inch the no-nonsense business tycoon. "May I see you in the hallway for a moment, Jenny?"

While brother and sister left, Samantha remained at the table and finished her milk.

Hugh stood across the room, pruning fern leaves with a small pair of scissors.

"They're beautiful," she said. "The ferns, I mean."

He smiled at her. "Thanks, Samantha."

"The plants are important to you, aren't they?"

Hugh nodded. "If I weren't the Randalls' housekeeper, I'd work in a greenhouse. If I weren't lying in a ditch somewhere, that is."

Samantha made a questioning sound, curious but hesitant to pry.

"I was a practicing alcoholic when Beth found me fifteen years ago," he explained. "She helped me get sober, then offered me a job...."

Jenny popped back into the breakfast room. "Ready?"

Samantha rose, automatically gathering the empty

glasses in her hand. She realized she had no idea where to put them.

Hugh appeared by her side. "I'd be happy to take those from you, Samantha."

She relinquished her burden, but noticed she felt odd being waited on—which only confirmed her suspicion that this wealthy life-style wasn't what she'd known as a child. She must have taken a giant step up the financial ladder by marrying into the Randall family.

At the door Jenny linked her arm through Samantha's. "Garrick made me promise to be good," she said, obviously amused. "I'm allowed to give you a brief tour of the house, just enough so you won't get lost, and leave you alone to rest. And he says I'm supposed to let you remember things on your own."

"Why?"

"I don't know. He said the doctor agreed, but he didn't explain the reasons. It doesn't make sense to me, though. I mean, if you know things, but just don't remember you know them, then why shouldn't we tell you what you already know? It couldn't do any harm, could it?"

"I guess not."

Jenny gave a theatrical sigh. "But we have to follow the master's orders—not a word about the past. The kitchen is down that hallway, by the way. Hugh won't mind if you raid the refrigerator. You and he are good friends." She clapped a hand to her mouth. "I shouldn't have said that."

"It's okay, Jenny. I'd figured that out, anyway. I was scared of him at first, but I'm not anymore."

Jenny blinked at her, then shook her head. "Gosh, that's so weird."

"Why?" she asked. What was strange about being scared of a man who looked like Frankenstein's monster?

"You said those exact same words ten years ago. The first time you met Hugh, you practically ran screaming from the house. But pretty soon you guys were buddies. And now you repeated the same thing you told me then. Amnesia's pretty wild, isn't it, Sam?"

She nodded. "Garrick said I wanted to be called Samantha."

Jenny rolled her eyes. "Well, if that isn't just like Garrick, saying whatever he wants about your past while forbidding me to do the same! So what if you *did* ask to be called Samantha? You like Sam better. Samantha was just an attempt to sound sophisticated because— Well, never mind why. You like to be called Sam, so that's what I'm going to call you."

Samantha didn't see any sense in arguing, since she had no idea which name she normally liked better. Sam sounded fine for the time being.

True to her word, Jenny led her on a brief but thorough tour of the important parts of the house, ignoring the east wing and the third floor entirely. By the time she deposited her at her bedroom door, Samantha felt reasonably confident she could find her way downstairs again, and utterly frustrated that she couldn't remember a thing about a house she'd apparently known quite well.

Aside from that fleeting memory of her mother and the strange moment of familiarity in the entrance hall when Jenny had run down to greet her, she was still no closer to regaining her past.

Jenny gave her another hug. "You should rest now, just as his lordship ordered. I'll be reading up for my next exam if you need me. Garrick's probably closeted in his study, though I'm sure he'll come check on you before long, and Mom will be home for lunch in a couple hours." She kissed her on the cheek. "It's great to have you home, Sam. We really missed you."

Samantha closed the heavy wood door to the bedroom as Jenny started down the hallway. She looked around herself, taking in the high ceiling with its stucco designs, the ornately carved four-poster bed, the elegant dressing table and the lush Chinese carpet under her feet. It all exuded wealth.

And Samantha hated it.

Chapter Three

She swept her gaze through the bedroom again. Admittedly, it was beautiful. Most people would be thrilled to have such a room.

Samantha wasn't.

Perhaps foolishly, she'd hoped she and Garrick would share a room—but this luxurious haven was clearly hers and hers alone. Samantha couldn't find a single indication of masculine occupancy. The feminine items were obvious, though: potpourri and scented candles; a flacon of perfume on the dressing table, along with a vase of blue irises; something long and silky hanging from a hook on the door to the private bath.

Stepping farther into the room, she wondered which items should look familiar. If they'd told her she'd lived here a decade instead of two months, she'd never have been the wiser. Everything looked equally foreign.

She lifted the perfume stopper and held it under her nose, then grimaced. The scent was sexy and cloying, and no doubt expensive, but it didn't appeal to her. It was something a wealthy young woman would wear to a charity auction.

Sighing heavily, Samantha stashed the perfume in the dressing table drawer. This room confirmed her worst fears about herself. She doubted she'd have accepted a separate bedroom—no matter how lavish—if she'd married for love rather than money.

At least they had a connecting door, she told herself. A small consolation.

She crossed to the opening and gazed through it, feeling like a spy, but unable to stop herself. Garrick's room had simpler furniture, darker colors and a solid, no-nonsense, king-size bed. And, in some elusive way, it smelled different. Spicier. More masculine, like Garrick himself.

Samantha closed her eyes, inhaling deeply as if she'd been drowning and finally made it onto dry land. Then she realized what she was doing and felt like an idiot.

Stepping back from the doorway, she finished her exploration. She learned the locations of her clothes—which were blessedly simple and unpretentious, including her business attire—and blushed when she came to the lingerie chest. She might be modest on the outside, but on the inside she seemed to be quite the romantic.

Too bad her marriage had nothing to do with romance.

Enough! she thought. She had to stop moping, stop feeling sorry for herself. She'd gotten herself into this marriage—even though she couldn't remember doing it—and she'd have to deal with the consequences.

Samantha showered and lay down for a while, remembering Dr. Hernandez's warning to take it easy. Her hands kept returning to her belly, and she wondered how long it would take before the pregnancy really showed.

She felt better when she thought about the baby. Despite her current uncertainty, she knew she loved it very much. Tenderness swept through her every time she imagined holding her child in her arms. And if she was capable of such loving feelings, then maybe she wasn't such a conniving person after all....

At half past twelve, Garrick knocked on her door to announce lunch was ready.

"Get settled in?" he asked when she joined him in the hall.

"Yes, thank you." She met his gaze, her mind full of questions. Does that door between our rooms stay open each night? Do we ever sleep together? Just what sort of arrangement is this?

But she didn't ask, as if the answers would be carved in stone once he'd spoken them. She wasn't quite ready for that.

Downstairs in the dining room, Samantha met Beth Randall. *Met* wasn't the right word, of course, since she'd obviously known the older woman for years, but Samantha couldn't think of any other way to express it: once again she confronted a face she didn't recognize.

"Don't worry," Beth said in a kindly voice. "I understand all about your memory lapse. I'm sure things will feel strange to you for a while, but that will pass."

Hugh served a rich tomato soup with fresh-baked bread, followed by herbed roast chicken. After a mediocre breakfast at the hospital, Samantha had a healthy appetite—not to mention the fact that she was eating for two.

She enjoyed speaking with her mother-in-law. Beth was open, warm, and friendly. An older version of Jenny, Beth had short dark hair and an attractive middle-aged figure. Jenny had obviously inherited her enthusiasm and bright blue eyes from her mother, but in both aspects Beth had a quality of wisdom and serenity that Jenny hadn't yet developed.

Beth was a partner in a Portland law firm specializing in antidiscrimination law. Currently she was preparing for a major case, and Samantha soon realized that having Beth home for lunch was more a special occasion than an everyday event. She felt touched that Beth had taken time out of her day to welcome her home.

During the meal, Beth told them about her case and generally steered the conversation to topics that would be of interest even to an amnesiac. Everyone behaved naturally, Samantha thought, as if it were perfectly normal to sit down to lunch with someone who didn't even know her own identity.

They were a loving family. But she still felt like an outsider. She didn't remember any of them, and couldn't help wondering if she were only sitting at the table because she'd manipulated her way into their household.

At the end of the meal, Jenny and Hugh cleared the table together. Beth Randall drew Samantha aside and said to Garrick, "I'm going to take your wife out to the garden for a minute. That is," she said, turning to Samantha, "if you feel up to a short stroll?"

"I'd like that," she replied, though she felt a moment's unease. This had the look of a serious conversation. How much did Beth know about her son's marriage? And how much had she guessed about Samantha's motives?

They walked out through the French doors at the back of the house and wandered through the sculpted garden to a bench overlooking the city below.

On the bench Beth turned to face her and took her hands in hers. "This must be very difficult for you," she said, "waking up to a strange family and being married to a man you don't recognize."

Samantha nodded.

Beth squeezed her hands. "You may not remember it, but we all love you very much. This is your home, and you would be welcome here even if you weren't married to my son."

"Oh..." At Beth's expression of support, tears

prickled Samantha's eyes. She felt so confused and turned around by the events of the past day.

"I've tried to be a mother for you since your parents died," Beth continued. "And I love you as much as if you were my own daughter."

Samantha's chest constricted. Could Beth love her if she'd manipulated Garrick into marriage, and done it only for the money? She doubted the older woman, who seemed so wise and perceptive, would misjudge her character to such an extent.

Samantha thought again of her feelings for her baby. She remembered the warm and affectionate welcomes everyone had given her.

Maybe, just maybe, Beth loved her because she was a good person. Maybe she hadn't done all the things she imagined she had.

"I'm sure Garrick and Jenny will take great care of you," Beth said. "But if you do need someone else to talk with, call me at the office anytime." She glanced at her watch and stood up. "I'm sorry to run off, but I have to get back downtown."

Just inside the French doors, Beth gave her a hug. "I'm so glad you weren't hurt in the accident, Samantha. And I'm glad you finally married Garrick. There's no one else I'd rather welcome into the family, and I can't tell you how excited I am to be a grandmother soon."

Samantha didn't know how long she stood there, staring into space, after Beth had left.

At one point she felt Garrick's hand on her shoulder and turned to find him standing beside her. "Samantha?" he asked. "You okay?"

She nodded, looking up into his eyes. "I'm fine."

He examined her face closely. "You look as if you've been crying."

"I haven't." She'd come close, outside with Beth, but she didn't say so. "I'm just feeling a little emotional." She tried to smile. "Pregnant ladies are like that."

Garrick led her down the hall to the library. He closed the door behind them and sat her down on a soft leather sofa.

"Samantha," he said, reaching out to brush a strand of hair behind her ear, "tell me what's wrong."

She shook her head. "Nothing's wrong."

"Did my mother say something to upset you?"

She shook her head again, causing the strand of hair to come loose. "She said she loves me," she admitted, her voice catching.

And then she burst into tears.

Garrick drew her into his arms, letting her sob on his shoulder. He wrapped one arm tightly around her waist, and with the other hand stroked her back in a comforting motion.

It felt wonderful just to be held in his arms, to have his warmth envelop her and be able to depend on his strength. She shifted to get closer, burrowing against him. She surrendered to all the chaotic emotions within her, all the fear, loneliness and confusion. All the doubts and self-recriminations.

Garrick just held her tightly against him until her tears stopped falling. She felt his lips against her skin and hair, and realized he was giving her gentle kisses.

She didn't want the kisses to stop, but finally she released her grip on his strong shoulder and pushed herself back upright. "I've ruined your shirt."

Garrick shook his head. He brushed back her hair and wiped away her tears with the pad of his thumb.

She stared into his eyes, amazed at his tenderness toward her. How could she have ever thought his gray eyes were hard? They weren't hard at all, but soft and soothing. Filled with compassion and, if she didn't know better, something that looked an awful lot like love.

Their gazes held for a long moment. Then his dropped slowly to her mouth and he bent his head to kiss her lips.

The caress was warm and soft, sending cascades of liquid languor running through her. Garrick kept kissing her, gently, until she closed her eyes and relaxed back against him. And then he simply held her cradled against him for a long, long time.

Samantha spent the rest of the afternoon in the garden, reading books on pregnancy. Garrick had installed her on the patio outside his private study, and though she couldn't see him through the reflections on the glass, his nearness comforted her.

She felt better. Crying her heart out on Garrick's shoulder had done wonders for her state of mind. She'd been bottling up all the terror and uncertainty of waking up in a hospital not knowing who she was—and then coming home to an unexpected mansion—and it was a blessed relief to give in to those emotions.

She was beginning to feel safer. Beth and Jenny loved her, and whatever Garrick might or might not feel, she now knew he didn't despise her—he couldn't, and still be capable of the tenderness he'd shown after her talk with Beth.

Jenny joined her for a while to read one of her law textbooks, and Garrick came out frequently with snacks and glasses of juice, each time staying to chat a few minutes.

Maybe, she thought when she was alone again, maybe the story behind her marriage wasn't as sordid as she'd imagined. What if, instead of scheming to marry Garrick, she'd simply fallen victim to a momentary passion? They'd been friends for years, he'd told her. Didn't friendship sometimes change abruptly between men and women?

If so, they'd obviously been careless, and for the sake of their child, had agreed to marry. Maybe their friendship would be enough to keep them happy.

She looked up as Garrick stepped out onto the patio, a small bunch of grapes in his hand. "How are you feeling?" he asked.

She stared at the grapes. "Full."

He laughed, his gray eyes sparkling. "Pregnant women are supposed to eat well—and frequently. You have to put on enough weight for the baby to be healthy."

"It's not a question of the weight, Garrick," she answered, grinning back at him. "My stomach just isn't big enough after all the crackers and fruit and juice you've been feeding me this afternoon."

"Mind if I eat these grapes, then?"

"Not at all."

He pulled up a chair and relaxed down onto it. They sat together in the warm spring air. She read a few pages while Garrick ate the grapes.

It was difficult to concentrate with him sitting so near. Her eyes kept drifting toward his lips and jaw, toward the long nimble fingers transporting grapes to his mouth.

He had kissed her. This husband of hers who didn't love her—but who seemed to like and care for her— had kissed her and stroked her face with his fingers. He had kissed her lightly, fleetingly, and she'd wanted more.

She was definitely attracted to him. It was easy to imagine that after years of friendship with this handsome man, she'd begun to feel an overwhelming desire for him. She certainly felt it now. And look what happened! She was reduced to reading baby books and trying to keep her eyes off his impossibly sexy mouth.

"Anything interesting?" he asked.

Her gaze flew to his. Had he caught her staring?

"In the book," he said. "Which one is that, anyway?"

She closed the book, using her finger to keep her place, and tilted the cover toward him.

"Oh, that one's pretty intimidating." He leaned down and selected a book from the stack by her chair. "This one is a lot more pleasant. We both liked it the best."

"You've read all these?" She shouldn't have been surprised, she guessed.

Garrick grinned. "And a few more, too. I'm probably as overwhelmed by the whole pregnancy thing as you are. Do you want the last grape?"

She did, she realized. Her tongue was already anticipating the sweetness of it. "Sure," she said, striving for nonchalance. "If you don't."

She held out her hand, but he ignored it. Instead, he raised his hand to her lips, the grape held between his thumb and forefinger.

Their eyes met as the grape touched her lips. Samantha felt a jolt of awareness at the fascination in Garrick's gaze. Quickly she took the grape into her mouth and looked away. When she looked back, the fascination was gone.

But it had been there, she assured herself when he'd left. She hadn't imagined it. And it was easy to believe they might have been swept away by mutual passion three months ago.

She still felt confused about the circumstances. But since she wouldn't know everything until she got her memory back—*if* she got her memory back—she resolved on the spot to do all she could to make her marriage a good one. Though she may have gotten into it for bad or careless reasons, she had no plans to get out of it. Garrick was a warm and caring man, and his family loved her. Maybe he would grow to love her, too.

She knew she could grow to love him.

Garrick sat in bed, wearing his dressing gown and a pair of pajama bottoms, with a marketing report on his lap. He tried to focus on the important information in front of him but kept thinking of his wife.

Just as he had all afternoon.

With Samantha reading baby books outside his study window, he hadn't gotten a thing done. He couldn't keep his mind off that kiss they'd shared—that *first* kiss, though she didn't know it.

Ten years, he thought, and they'd only kissed once. Even at their civil ceremony two months ago he'd only brushed his lips against her cheek.

He could still taste the salt of her tears, could still feel her breasts pressed against his chest and her warm breath on his skin. He'd needed every ounce of self-control not to bend her back on the couch and take her right there.

And all he'd been able to think about all afternoon was how it would feel to peel her shirt up over her head, unhook her bra and feel her skin against his own.

After dinner that evening, he'd taken refuge in his study while Jenny and Samantha watched one of the old black-and-white movies they liked so much, but he'd managed to compose only one business letter in almost two hours. He'd finally given up and found them just as the video ended.

The three of them had spent a companionable hour together, easing into a familiar pattern: he and Samantha worked on a jigsaw puzzle while Jenny read aloud to them from an old gothic novel.

It had been both bliss and torment. It was bliss just to be with her, to sit across the table from her and work on the puzzle together, listening to Jenny's dramatic intonations. It was torment to accidentally brush her hand when reaching to fit a piece into place.

Countless times he'd ended up staring at her, at the way she bit her bottom lip and tapped her chin with a puzzle piece as she searched for the spot where it should go.

Jenny had caught him looking and, each time, had given him a knowing little smile without once interrupting her reading. He'd finally had to excuse himself and come upstairs to bed, tired of putting himself through the strain of being so close to his wife.

Now she was near him again. She'd entered her room a minute ago and headed straight for her private bath. He could hear water running in the sink as she got ready for bed.

He should have closed the connecting door when he'd had the chance. He'd noticed it was open right away, of course, but he'd convinced himself that closing it would make her feel rejected.

It was much too late now. To close the door, he'd have to step into her room. With his luck, she'd come out of the bathroom right then, and he'd have to see her soft brown eyes fill with confusion and hurt. Even if she didn't catch him doing it, she'd still feel the weight of his rejection.

And the last thing he wanted to do was reject his sweet, desirable wife.

So he left the door standing open.

Having her this close was more difficult than he'd imagined. It had been difficult before her accident, too, knowing she was sleeping on the other side of the wall. But at least they'd both known the ground rules then: the door stayed closed until some unknown time in the future when they *might* decide to change their relationship. When they might decide to be more than friends, and make their marriage a real one.

Now everything was in flux, and it was as uncomfortable for him as it must be for Samantha.

His eyes strayed to the framed photograph on his bedside table. Jenny had put it there, he knew, just as she must have opened the connecting door, which usually stayed firmly shut. Jenny, the unswerving matchmaker, who'd guessed how he felt a long time ago.

The picture was exactly the one he would have chosen for his bedside table. Taken a few months before his father had died, it showed himself and Samantha in the kitchen, looking for all the world like a man and woman in love. Garrick was gazing at her as if she looked good enough to eat, and Samantha herself was laughing, her head thrown back and her eyes sparkling.

He remembered that afternoon well. What he'd said to her hadn't even been that funny, something about a course she'd taken at the university, but the camera had captured the scene as if they were the only two people in the world who could ever make each other happy.

And for him at least, it was true. No one else could make him feel so excited and alive, no matter how tired he was, or how frustrated he was with the rest of his life.

He'd been twenty-four at the time of the photo. Just a few years out of college. Warren had been off jet-setting again, doing his best to make sure their father wouldn't retire and saddle him with the company and real responsibilities. And Garrick had been working hard to cover up for Warren's absence.

As usual.

Garrick felt the old bitterness rise up inside him, but quickly tamped it down. That was all over now. Warren could no longer hurt any of them. It was pointless and petty to cling to all the old grievances.

With an effort Garrick pulled his thoughts from the past and applied his attention to the marketing report.

He didn't get far before Samantha appeared in the doorway between their rooms, still dressed in a T-shirt and jeans. Her hair was down, as it had been for most of the day, and the light from her room gave it a golden glow around her face.

He hadn't realized until this moment how much he'd missed seeing her hair down around her shoulders. In recent years she'd worn it piled on her head in chignons and twists, thinking those styles made her look more sophisticated.

"Hi," he said, wondering if she'd come to close the door between their rooms.

"Hi," she said. "What are you reading?"

"A marketing report." He smiled.

"What's so amusing?"

"Sorry. I was just thinking how bizarre this is." He held out the report so she could see the cover. "You wrote most of it."

She squinted across the room. "I did? Really? Let me see." She crossed to the side of his bed, her hand out.

He gave her the report, then watched as she thumbed through it.

She looked beautiful. Her skin was fresh and clean and smooth, clear of makeup. Her hair was wet along her hairline from washing her face, and one drop of water had run down her neck to make a spot of dampness on the collar of her shirt.

She sat on the edge of the bed, as if it were the most natural thing in the world. "I really wrote this?" she asked.

"Yes, and it's good."

He could smell her scent, as he had when she'd cried in his arms, and later when they'd worked on the puzzle. But in the dimly lit space of his bedroom it was all the more overpowering. She smelled of delicate rose petals and of herself, and it reminded him of the time in the photograph, when Samantha had been just Sam. How long had it been since she'd smelled this way? Not more than a few years, but it seemed like forever that she'd been wearing that other perfume that Warren had given her.

The urge to reach out a hand and draw his wife up against him was almost too powerful to resist. Did she have even the slightest clue what she was doing to him by walking into his bedroom and planting herself on his bed?

She pointed to a paragraph of the report. "Is this what I do all day? Conduct focus groups and then write reports?"

"You do all sorts of things. You're our best facilitator, though, so you do a lot of that." He couldn't believe she was in his bedroom—his *bedroom,* for goodness sake—and they were discussing business.

She flipped through a few more pages, then sighed. "Well, I'll definitely have to wait for my memory to return before going back to work. This stuff all makes sense, but there's no way I'd be able to do it on my own."

"Give it time. I'm sure everything will come back eventually." And, he realized, he dreaded that moment.

She nodded. "I think that's what it's going to take." She gave him the report, then caught sight of the picture on his bedside table. "May I see that?"

He handed her the photograph.

She looked at it closely for several seconds. "How old was I when this was taken?"

"Nineteen."

"In college, right? I look so young." She glanced up, meeting his gaze. In her eyes he could see that mixture of uncertainty and trust. But now there was also hopefulness in her brown eyes. "You keep this on your bedside table," she said, her voice filled with a sort of satisfied wonderment.

What could he say? *No, my interfering sister put it there?* "It's a nice picture," he managed to say. "I like it."

"I do, too," she said. "We've been friends a long time, haven't we?"

"Ten years."

"There's a similar picture in my room. We're both younger, but we look the same, if you know what I mean."

He nodded, thinking that his sister had been nothing if not thorough. He wondered what other little surprises he and Samantha might find hidden around their rooms. Condoms in the nightstand, perhaps? Not that they would need them, of course.

Samantha handed back the photo. "Kinda gives you hope for our marriage, doesn't it?"

His jaw almost dropped. This was Samantha, his beautiful, sexy wife, saying their future looked bright? "Yes," he said, his mouth having difficulty with the word. "Yes, it does."

She stood and crossed back to the open door. "Well, I have to finish getting ready for bed."

Then she was gone, as if she'd never been there. Except he could still smell rose petals and see the impression left in the bed by her delectable body.

Thank God for amnesia, he thought madly, feeling his heartbeat quicken. Everything was going to work out. It might still take time, but eventually Samantha would realize everything their relationship could be. And when that time came, he'd be right here waiting for her.

A few minutes passed. He put away her marketing report, tossed his robe onto a chair and turned out the bedside light. He knew he wouldn't be able to sleep, not for a long time.

"When do you wake up?" Samantha called from the other room.

He loved the huskiness of her voice, Garrick thought. "Five-thirty. Usually."

"Five-thirty? Good heavens."

"You do, too," he told her.

"I do?"

He started to nod, forgetting she couldn't see. "Well, you have since we got married."

She poked her head around the doorway, smiling sheepishly. Her shoulder was bare. "I guess that makes sense."

Garrick stared for a moment, his hormones kicking in. There was no particular reason why the sight of his wife's bare neck and shoulder should drive him wild, but it did. Knowing she was shirtless and braless behind the connecting wall was almost too much for him. "We...we drive in together," he managed in a strangled voice.

"Oh, of course," she said, disappearing again. "Are you going to work tomorrow?"

He knew he should, if only because he wasn't going to get anything done at home. "No," he said. "I'm going to stay here with you, just as I did today."

And I'm going to go slowly crazy, he thought, *until you finally fall in love with me.*

"So we can sleep in, right? They say pregnant women need a lot of rest."

"I read that, too. If I have to get up early, I'll try to be quiet."

"Good," she said.

The lights went out in her room.

He stared into the darkness for a minute, wondering why he didn't hear the sound of the bedsprings creaking in her room.

"Good night," he called.

"You don't have to yell," Samantha answered from the doorway. "I'm right here."

Then he heard footsteps. Soft, padding footsteps, the sound of bare feet on a thick rug. He sensed her presence, picked up the scent of rose petals as she moved through the room.

Garrick stared, catching just a glimpse of a flowing white nightgown as she circled the foot of his bed and slipped between the sheets.

Oh, good Lord, he thought. Now he was really in trouble.

Chapter Four

Samantha pulled the covers to her chin. She squirmed to get comfortable, twisting the filmy nightgown around her legs. After reaching down to straighten the fabric, she glanced over at her husband.

A foot or two away, his shape was a large silhouette in the darkness. He'd levered up on an elbow, as if to get a better vantage point. Samantha couldn't make out his expression, but she knew he watched her.

She closed her eyes and snuggled back against the pillow, and said as normally as she could, "Good night, Garrick. Sleep well...."

He was silent for a long moment. Finally he lowered his torso back to the mattress. The bed shifted gently underneath him. "Good night, Samantha."

The room was so quiet she could hear his lashes

brush the pillowcase every time he blinked. Why didn't he close his eyes and go to sleep?

Samantha felt her courage falter. Was she crazy to do this, to climb uninvited into her husband's bed? Had any wife ever done anything more foolish?

Her fears had been correct, she thought. She didn't belong here.

But there was no going back. She'd crossed the line when she'd entered his room wearing only a wispy silk nightgown—even if it *was* the most modest one she seemed to own—and to retreat now would be humiliating. She'd already taken the risk and had to see it through. And, she told herself, the risk would be worthwhile if it brought them closer together. If it strengthened their marriage.

Samantha breathed in deeply. Garrick's compelling male scent clung to the ultrasoft sheets, wrapping her in an intimate cocoon of awareness. She could feel his heat alongside her, drawing her toward him like a magnet.

This wasn't so bad, she told herself. There were worse fates than finding oneself in bed with a gorgeous husband in the prime of his manhood.

Sure, the air was a little tense. It seemed to hum between them. But that was understandable. Her senses were heightened by her tumultuous emotions and the unusual situation.

Thinking a brief conversation might ease the strain, Samantha searched her mind for something to say.

She turned onto her side, facing him. "Garrick?"

"Hmmm?"

"You're staying home tomorrow, right?"

"Yes."

"How soon will you have to go back to work?"

"I'll stay here as long as you need me," he said. "Until you're better, if necessary."

She thought she heard a touch of frustration and wondered if staying home with her was keeping him from something important. "It's okay if you need to go to the office. I mean, if you have stuff to do..."

"It's no problem, Samantha."

"Oh." It didn't sound as if it were no problem. She opened her eyes, trying to read his expression in the dark. "You don't mind watching over me?" she asked.

"Not at all."

"It doesn't interfere with your work?"

Garrick didn't answer at first. He shifted his position on the bed, which tugged the covers toward him, which made her silk nightgown slide against her skin. It left a shimmery sensation in her nerve endings.

"No," he said finally. "I'm just as productive here as I am in the office."

Samantha lay still, absorbing her body's response. She liked being this close to him, she thought, liked being aware of his every movement. It made her feel very...wifely.

"That's good," she said.

"Yes, it is." Garrick adjusted his pillow.

She bit her lip, then said, "You're trying to sleep, aren't you?"

"Trying," he agreed.

She thought she heard a smile in his voice. "I guess we don't usually chat before going to sleep, do we?"

"Not usually," he answered.

His wry tone of voice made her pulse speed up— it made her think of what else they might do before falling asleep.

Make love. If *that* was their usual bedtime activity, then of course Garrick wouldn't want to talk. Not when there was a much more interesting means of communication available.

"Sorry," she said, wondering what it would feel like to climb into bed and have Garrick pull her into his arms, have him caress her through the sheer fabric of her nightgown.

"Sorry for what?" Garrick said.

Samantha closed her eyes, glad he couldn't see her in the darkness. She had to get a grip on herself! "For not remembering."

"It's okay," he said. "You have amnesia."

"I'm sorry about that, too."

"Don't be. It was an accident."

"I know, but I feel bad for it, anyway, and for making you take care of me. It must be difficult to have a wife who doesn't remember—" She swallowed. "Who doesn't remember being with you before. I feel as if I've turned your whole life upside down."

"It's all right, Samantha. I'm getting used to it."

"I—I guess I should let you sleep," she said uncertainly.

Garrick rolled onto his back and readjusted the sheets. He muttered something she didn't quite catch.

"What was that?"

Garrick sighed. "Nothing." He sighed again. "I just said I doubt I'll be able to sleep much tonight."

Samantha bent her knees, still facing him. She hugged them to her chest. "Would you rather I went back to my room?"

Garrick made a husky sound that wasn't quite a laugh, more an ironic rumble. It caressed her ears, and she shivered a little.

"To be totally honest," he said, "I like having you in my bed."

At the possessive way he said the words, heat flashed through her. "You do?" she asked, sounding breathless.

"Yes. But you should be wherever you're most comfortable."

Samantha pictured the queen-size bed next door. The crisp, fresh sheets and sumptuous bedspread would still be cold, she thought. They wouldn't carry Garrick's subtle scent or wrap her in an intimate cocoon.

She probably wouldn't have any more chance of sleeping in that foreign-feeling room, she told herself. Here, at least, she was with her husband, and even though she didn't remember him, he'd begun to be familiar.

"I guess I'll stay here, then," she said.

But twenty minutes later, having cycled through several restless positions, Samantha was still wide awake. No matter what she did, no matter how she tried to distract herself, she couldn't curb her awareness of Garrick.

She wondered if he wore anything beneath the sheets. When she'd come to look at the marketing report, he'd worn some kind of robe—rich slate gray, a few shades deeper than his eyes, elegant and masculine. But wouldn't he have taken it off in order to sleep? And had there been anything underneath?

If she merely reached across the bed, Samantha thought, she could find out.

A dangerous little thrill ran down her spine. She wondered what he'd look like in the morning, with his dark hair all tousled from sleep.

And she wondered what he'd do if she kissed him.

Samantha remembered their embrace that afternoon. Though intense, it had also been comforting and tentative, as if they were delicately exploring each other for the first time. In a way, of course, it had been their first kiss—at least from her perspective. Garrick could be familiar with her lips to the point of boredom, but to her, his every plane and angle was like a new land to be explored and mapped and conquered....

Samantha rolled onto her side once more. She stared at Garrick's profile in the dim light that filtered through the windows on either side of the bed. Her eyes had adjusted to the dark, so she could see that his eyes were closed. His profile was handsome and strong, his chin well defined, his lips full and sensuous.

And, as far as she could tell, he was still awake. His breathing hadn't settled into a regular rhythm, and every few minutes he moved around, as if he couldn't get comfortable.

"Garrick?" she asked softly.

At first she thought he hadn't heard her, but then she saw his eye open. "Garrick?" she repeated.

No answer.

Samantha bit her lip. She shouldn't have said anything, she realized. She should have just lain there until exhaustion finally overcame the heady sensations of being in Garrick's bed. "Forget it," she said. "Go back to sleep."

He rolled his head on the pillow and seemed to fix his eyes on her face. In the dim light she could barely make out his expression. He didn't look particularly happy.

Finally he closed his eyes as if he were in pain and turned his face back to the ceiling.

She heard him give a muffled groan.

"What's wrong?" she asked.

"Nothing's wrong." He swung an arm over his eyes.

She watched, trying to understand his reaction. "Something's wrong, Garrick. I'm your wife. You can tell me."

He turned toward her and levered up on an elbow, just as he'd done when she'd climbed into bed. The bedclothes lifted with his movement; cool air drifted down between them.

Goose bumps tightened her skin. She felt exposed

suddenly, as if he could see her naked body beneath the nightgown. It wasn't a frightening feeling—just a little uncomfortable, with a return of that shimmery sensation, as if a small electric current were dancing across her flesh.

"What could possibly be wrong, Samantha?"

"I don't know," she said.

He laughed, but didn't seem amused. It was a rough, self-mocking laugh. "What, indeed. You're here in my bed, where you belong, wearing a nightgown that would tempt a saint. Nothing's wrong. Nothing at all."

She still felt confused, but latched on to the small measure of reassurance she found in his words. "I belong in your bed?"

No answer.

"I'm welcome here?"

"Yes, Samantha.... You're welcome in my bed."

Pleasure filled her, unexpected in its intensity. "Good," she said. "With the amnesia and all, I guess I wasn't sure... I'm so glad. And I'm glad the amnesia hasn't changed anything. I mean, it shouldn't, right? It's just a little memory loss." She was babbling, she realized, but couldn't seem to stop. "It doesn't change the fact that we're husband and wife...."

"Go to sleep, Samantha."

"I can't," she admitted, fidgeting with the covers, folding the edge of the sheet back and forth between her fingers like an accordion. She sighed. "Too worked up, I guess."

"Well, you should try, anyway," he growled. "I need to get some rest tonight, and you're keeping me from it."

Her brows drew together. "Are you angry with me, Garrick?"

"No, I'm not angry with you, Samantha."

"Then what's going on...? You can't sleep. Okay, why not? Tell me."

Silence.

He said, "I can't sleep because you're in bed with me. I don't want to sleep. I want to make love with you. Slowly. I want to drown in the rose petal scent of you, want to push aside that flimsy little nightgown and caress every inch of your body until you melt in my arms. And then I want to slip inside you and bring us both the release we damn well deserve. That's why I can't sleep, Samantha. Is that what you wanted to hear?"

She couldn't breathe. His words, rough as they were, sent a wave of liquid heat crashing through her body. She felt them like a physical touch, a seductive stroke of his fingers on her skin.

Yes, she realized, those words were exactly what she wanted to hear. She wanted him to do all those things he'd described, to welcome her home as only a husband could.

But she couldn't bring herself to say that, so she said something else instead. "You...you don't have to call me Samantha if you don't want to."

Garrick stared at her. "What?" He sounded as if he was choking.

"You can call me Sam. I don't remember why I liked Samantha, but I think I like Sam better."

Silence descended on the room, and it lasted so long she wondered if Garrick had suddenly fallen asleep. He didn't move a muscle. The sheets didn't rustle and the bedsprings didn't shift. She could hear the distant creaking sounds as the old mansion settled down for the night.

Finally she found the courage to look at his face.

Garrick's incredulity was clear even in the dim light. "Didn't you hear a word I said?"

"I heard you just fine," she answered. He might have meant to scare her off, but he'd only done the opposite. He'd piqued her curiosity. Now she wanted to feel his lips on hers, feel his hands touching her.

"I heard you just fine," she repeated.

He gave a groan of frustration. "And?"

"And okay."

He was absolutely still.

"I said okay, Garrick. You can make love to me if you want to."

Garrick switched on the light.

She blinked at him in the sudden glare. He stared back at her, and she thought she saw a heat in his gray eyes to match the heat in her body, but she couldn't be sure.

His gaze roved over her face, then dipped lower to the swell of her breasts. The covers had slipped down to reveal them, and the sheer nightgown was no barrier at all. It only accentuated the sensual feel of her nipples as they tightened under Garrick's perusal.

Samantha made her own perusal, trailing her gaze across the bare skin of his shoulders and upper torso, taking note of the rock-hard muscles, wondering again what he wore farther down.

She caught her breath.

He made her feel sexy and desirable. He made her want him with a need that wiped out every other thought in her head. Had it been like this the first time? And the second and the third?

For a crazy moment Samantha actually savored her amnesia; it let her experience this overwhelming emotional and physical response to her husband as if it were their first time together.

She shivered, waiting.

But instead of drawing her into his warm embrace, Garrick pulled the covers back up to her chin. He adjusted them as if she were a child being tucked into bed. "Go to sleep, Sam."

For a moment she was so stunned she couldn't reply. She tried not to show her hurt. "Why?"

He shook his head regretfully. "Because we have to wait until you're better. As much as I'd like to make love with you tonight, you need to have your memory back first."

She didn't understand. And what if she *never* got her memory back? Would they never make love? "I'm your wife, Garrick. I'm having your baby. It's not as if we haven't done it before."

Garrick closed his eyes, shutting her out. When he opened them again, he seemed even more determined.

"I'm sorry, Sam, believe me. But it's just not possible."

He raised a hand to caress her face. His fingertips skimmed down her cheek, leaving a tingly trail in their wake. "We'll talk in the morning," he said gently. "Then you'll understand."

But she didn't think she would. What could he possibly say to explain his behavior, his rejection?

Garrick turned out the light and settled back on his side of the bed.

Samantha didn't speak.

It was going to be a very, very long night.

As soon as the sky began to lighten, Garrick eased out of bed. Quietly, so as not to wake his wife, he put on his robe, thinking of what he had to tell her—and trying to keep his eyes off her sleep-soft body.

Her golden hair fanned across the pillows. One bare arm lay atop the comforter. The warm yellow light of dawn washed over her, and he wanted more than anything to climb back into bed and curl his body around her.

He didn't want to tell her the truth.

Needing a chance to prepare himself, Garrick made his way downstairs for a cup of coffee. With any luck the rest of the household would still be asleep, and he'd have a few quiet moments alone before he faced the moment of reckoning.

He was out of luck. Jenny sat at the breakfast table poring over a law book, a glass of orange juice at her elbow.

"How's Sam?" she asked, glancing up.

Garrick went to the automatic coffeemaker on the sideboard and poured himself a cup. "She's fine."

Jenny gave him an amused look. "Well, aren't we cheery this morning! What's wrong, did she sleep in her own bed last night? I thought the open door would be enough of a hint, but I guess it was too subtle."

"It wasn't too subtle," he growled. "She slept in my bed last night."

"Oh." His sister beamed with satisfaction. "Well, after all, she is your wife...."

Garrick turned his back on her, stalking up to the mass of ferns and staring out the window. He took a long sip of coffee and tried to calm himself down. "Jenny, don't you think this has gone far enough? I appreciate your efforts to trick Samantha into falling in love with me, but it's time to stop. When she wakes up, I'm going to remind her she doesn't love me. And doesn't want me as a husband." He turned around and met her eyes. "It isn't fair to keep her in the dark."

Jenny closed her law book with a thud. "What exactly happened last night, Garrick?"

He exhaled forcefully. "Exactly what you hoped would happen. Sam climbed into my bed, dressed in one of those obscene things I'm sure you planted in her room, and lay there waiting for me to make love to her."

Jenny gave him a disappointed look. "You didn't do it, did you?"

Garrick met her look with a scowl. His body ached

from spending so many hours so close to his desirable young wife, and it wasn't helping his mood. Neither was his lack of sleep. "In case you hadn't noticed," he said, "she's not herself. Wife or not, I could never take advantage of her like that."

Jenny considered him thoughtfully. "Maybe she's more herself than she has been in years. Is it so hard to believe she would actually desire you?"

Desire? He doubted that was the word for it.

You can make love to me if you want to, she'd said. Hardly a flattering invitation. Hardly an expression of consuming desire. More likely she'd resigned herself to doing her wifely duty.

He stared into his cup of coffee. "Desire isn't enough," he muttered.

"It's a start," Jenny said.

Garrick sighed and sat at the table. "Yes, a bad one. Look, Sam needs to know the truth. I'm going to tell her everything."

"Everything?"

"Yes, everything."

Jenny was quiet for a moment.

Garrick took advantage of her rare silence to take a few more sips of coffee. He watched her slowly twirl her glass of orange juice, staring into it as if it held the wisdom of the world.

At last she said, "I don't think that's a very good idea."

"I do."

She remained unfazed. "Yesterday," she mused, "you were the one telling *me* not to spill too much."

He folded his arms. "You weren't spilling facts, Jenny," he said, eyes narrowed. "You were spilling fabrications."

"Now, Garrick," she replied in a placating tone, "I know this is a confusing time for all of us. The trick is to keep your head. Letting your emotions rule everything will come to no good."

"And what is it you think I should do?"

Jenny stood and paced around the breakfast room, her steps measured and deliberate. She tilted her head. "It seems clear enough to me. Just go on as you have since Sam woke up. Continue to treat her as the wife you love very much, and don't breathe a word about the past—at least not about the important parts of the past."

"I can't hide her life from her, Jenny. I can't keep telling her half-truths and letting her jump to the wrong conclusions about everything."

"You don't have a choice," Jenny said. She stopped in her tracks and pointed an accusing finger at him. "What do you think will happen if you tell her the truth about the baby?"

His sister looked cool and calm and ruthless, Garrick thought. Like a lawyer making her closing arguments to the jury.

He said, "She knew the truth before the accident."

"Of course she did. But she doesn't know it now. All she knows is that she's married to a wonderful, caring, handsome man."

"And that she's pregnant."

"Right." Jenny came to stand in front of him, her

hands on her hips. "Which is exactly my point. She's in a delicate condition right now. I'm afraid the shock of learning how the baby was conceived, and how she came to be married to you, might be enough to cause a miscarriage."

He felt his chest tighten painfully. "Sam's made of stronger stuff than that."

"She's in a very confusing position, Garrick. She can't remember her past, and anything you tell her is going to have a powerful effect on her. Think about it. If she can't remember *everything* about the past ten years, the news of her recent actions will be a shock to her system."

"She wouldn't lose the baby."

Jenny stared down at him, then twisted the screw a final turn. "Are you so sure about that? Sure enough to risk the baby's life and Samantha's, too? Haven't we had enough trauma in the family?"

Garrick didn't answer. Just the thought of Samantha dying brought back the terrible panic he'd felt when the police had called to inform him of her car accident. His chest clenched tighter.

Jenny resumed her seat. She leaned forward across the table. Her voice was gentle. "You want that child, don't you?"

"Yes," he said. "I want the child. But I also want it to have a safe, loving home. I don't see how that's possible if its parents' marriage begins with this kind of deception."

"Tough. That's the risk you're going to have to take. The other alternative is unthinkable. So follow my advice and keep being the caring, loving husband I know you can be.''

''Dammit, Jenny.'' She was right. He didn't have a choice. And he hated being backed into a corner.

Jenny relaxed in her chair, a smile on her face. ''I know it's not ideal, Garrick. But look on the bright side. She might end up falling in love with you.''

Chapter Five

He'd said they would talk in the morning and then she would understand. But after their talk Samantha felt every bit as confused as she had before.

Garrick continued to insist they couldn't make love until she regained her memory. He said she needed more time to recover. She wasn't herself. Her state was too tenuous.

Something told Samantha the matter was more complex. And, though she knew it was probably better they hadn't rushed into intimacy on her first night back, she still felt that nagging sense of hurt.

That nagging, *familiar* sense of hurt, she realized with some surprise. Yes, it was familiar. Right around the edge of her consciousness hung the knowledge she'd felt that way before.

Well, that made sense, she told herself, especially

if she'd loved Garrick for the past ten years and he'd ignored her until recently. Maybe he'd been between girlfriends and had only turned to her for physical gratification—and maybe he felt so guilty for getting her pregnant that it made him reluctant to make love again.

It wasn't a pleasant thought.

To keep herself from brooding, Samantha spent the morning exploring the grounds, which included a tennis court and a swimming pool. Though her car had been scrapped after the wreck, and Beth and Jenny had left for the day, she found several vehicles in the converted carriage house—more evidence of the Randall family's wealth.

After lunch on the patio, she and Garrick cleaned up while Hugh ran errands. Watching her husband scrub a pan at the sink, Samantha thought again how attractive he was. He'd rolled up his white shirtsleeves, and a lock of dark hair had fallen over his forehead, making him look younger than usual. Almost as young as he was.

As they worked together, the tension between them ebbed. Garrick kept up a stream of conversation, describing the Rose Festival, Portland's annual citywide celebration, and suggesting they see a Broadway play that had recently come to town. Gradually Samantha forgot about his rejection the night before, charmed by his gentle teasing and lively gray eyes.

"Garrick," she said on impulse, "tell me more about yourself. I know that sounds strange," she added with a self-conscious laugh, "since we're married and having a baby..."

"What kinds of things would you like to hear about?"

"Anything and everything. I want to know you as well as I used to."

He rested his palms on the rim of the sink, turning his head to meet her gaze. "I don't want to tell you anything that might plant false memories."

"Then tell me stuff that has nothing to do with me. Tell me about your childhood. Tell me where you went to college. Have you always lived in this house?"

"You really want to know?"

When she nodded, he told her about the time he'd fallen out of the big maple tree in the back garden and broken his arm, about some of his more unruly escapades in high school and about his participation on the soccer and tennis teams in college.

"Do I play tennis?" she asked.

"Yes," he said, after a pause during which he obviously debated whether the information would hinder her recovery. "You and Jenny used to play a lot."

"Did I ever play with you?" She knew the question was off-limits, but asked it, anyway.

He grinned. "You're very good at tennis," he said, evading her question. "And a strong swimmer, too. Feel free to use the pool anytime you want."

"I don't suppose you're going to tell me if we used to swim together, either," she teased.

He shook his head. "I like to swim and you like

to swim, but that's all I'm going to say on the matter.''

''Then let's go swimming this afternoon.''

Garrick turned slowly toward her, his gaze skimming her figure before rising to her face. Was it her imagination, or did he linger over the swell of her breasts?

''I think,'' he said at last, ''that we should put that off until you're better.''

Until we can make love, Samantha thought, remembering their conversation from that morning. In her mind, getting better and being able to make love with her husband had become inextricably intertwined.

She also recalled the sexy bikini she'd found among her clothes. The very idea of wearing it in front of Garrick sent a wave of heat to her skin—the same feeling she got when she thought of slipping into bed with him that evening. Anticipation. Excitement. Longing.

Garrick had returned his attention to the basin of soapy water in front of him. She wasn't sure if he'd noticed the heat in her cheeks. Following his lead, she tried to focus on drying the dishes.

After she'd dried the last pan and set it on the counter, she tucked her hands into the pockets of her apron and watched Garrick rinse out the sink. The sight of him filled her with contentment, made her imagine a lifetime of sharing household tasks. In a year their baby would sleep nearby while they washed up. Six years from now, she thought with a smile, that same child might run wildly around the house while she and Garrick had a private moment in the kitchen.

Her smile faded as she imagined what Garrick might do during that private moment. Pull her into his arms, perhaps? Bury his hands in her hair and tantalize her with whispered images of what he would do to her later that evening? Or simply hold her close and kiss her?

"What are you thinking about?" Garrick asked softly.

She blinked up at him, refocusing her eyes. He'd stepped away from the sink to dry his hands on a towel. "Us," she said, then added quickly, "and our baby."

"Good thoughts?" He raised an inquiring eyebrow.

She blushed again, nodding. It was so easy to imagine the future with him. "I was thinking how nice it will be to be a family. The three of us." Or to be more than three—a family of four or five would be nice, too. She picked up one of the pans and dabbed at a drop of water she'd missed. She kept her eyes down. "Maybe we can have more children later...." Of course, more children meant making love again, which meant getting her memory back.

"I'd like that," Garrick said, his voice rough.

She looked up. "You would?"

"I've always wanted children." He hung up their towels, his glance taking in the stacks of dried pans. "You don't remember where they go?"

She shook her head.

"I'll show you." He reached around her for a large pot.

She picked up a saucepan and followed him across the kitchen to the cabinets beside Hugh's big restaurant-style range. "How many children?" she asked him.

"As many as you want. It's a big house."

"Two would be nice," she said a little wistfully. "Or three."

"I think we can manage that." He put the pans in the cabinet and went back to the sink.

She watched him, hoping he looked forward—as she did—to *making* the babies as well as raising them. "Did we already have this conversation?"

"No, we didn't." He handed her a frying pan. "This goes on the other side of the stove. Bottom shelf."

She slid it into place. "We never talked about having more kids?"

"We weren't thinking that far ahead." He tossed cooking utensils into a few different drawers, poured powdered soap into the dishwasher and switched it on. The machine came to life with a quiet hum.

"All finished," Garrick said, walking up to her. He reached around her to tug her apron strings loose, then raised his hands to lift the neck loop over her head.

She inhaled, smelling the lemony tang of dish soap that lingered on Garrick's hands. It mingled with the unmistakable scent of the man himself, spicy and very male.

His hand brushed against her hair, and something

shifted inside her. Languid desire pooled in her abdomen.

Surprised by the intensity of her response, she laid a hand on his chest. The fabric of his shirt was steamy and damp from standing over the hot dishwater. She felt the hard muscles of his chest underneath and thought she could even feel the solid pounding of his heart.

She stood there, her hand against his chest, aware that somewhere in the distant reaches of her mind, a memory had shaken itself loose. It descended slowly, like a tiny pebble bouncing down a cliff face, spinning lazily in the sunlight.

The images, hazy at first, gradually took on shape and depth. As clearly as if it had happened yesterday, she saw Garrick and Jenny roughhousing with her in the kitchen.

Jenny, a rambunctious sixteen, had started the nonsense, as usual. But it quickly escalated from playful snapping with twirled up towels to an all-out water fight. Puddles of water covered the floor.

In the memory Samantha was backed into a corner, held there by a very wet, very calm Garrick. His body blocked her escape, his hips pressing lightly against hers. The front of his shirt dripped soapy, citrus-scented water. She'd dipped both hands into the dishpan and doused him only moments before.

Remembering, Samantha drew in a sharp breath. Only Garrick's hips had touched her, but he'd raised a tall glass of water high above her head, well out of reach. Holding her gently prisoner, he'd slowly emptied the glass of water on the top of her head. Rivulets had run down her face and hair, soaking her shirt.

She'd gasped in shock, feeling the most amazingly physical sensations of surprise and confusion as she'd struggled to free herself from the corner, pushing against Garrick's strong adult body. The playfulness she'd felt earlier in their fight had disappeared, replaced not with fear but with emotions and sensations for which she'd had no name.

Then Garrick had muttered a sharp curse and abruptly jerked away, striding angrily from the room without a backward glance.

She'd been startled and confused by his withdrawal, and had felt the odd, uncomfortable feeling in her stomach slowly recede as the clammy fabric of her shirt brought her back to reality. She remembered Jenny looking at her with a curious expression, as if she, too, had seen something happen, but could no more identify it than Samantha could.

Desire, she thought now, as her breath came short and shallow. She might not have recognized the signs at sixteen, but she certainly did at twenty-five. What she'd felt that afternoon had been desire—raw, soul-deep desire.

And Garrick had obviously guessed it. Why else would he have spun away like that, his expression so closed and angry? After all, what twenty-one-year-old man would want to have a sixteen-year-old girl react to him that way?

Samantha frowned, slowly becoming aware that

during her memory Garrick had gathered her against him as if to hold her upright.

"Are you okay?" he asked her, concern in his voice. "You faded out on me for a second."

She released the handful of his shirt she'd clenched as the intensity of her memory swept over her. "I'm fine. I...I had a memory."

"A memory?" he echoed. His tone was suddenly level and calm. "Like the one of your mother?"

"No, clearer than that." She slipped her hand out from between them. "Crystal clear, actually. Nothing hazy about it. I remember what I saw, what I felt, what you said..."

"I was there?"

"Yes, you—" She broke off, shivering with remembered desire. *You were touching me,* she wanted to say, *pressing against me and arousing the most extraordinary sensations, just as you're doing now.* "Yes, you were there."

"Just you and me?"

"No."

"No?" His question was intent.

"Jenny was there, too. We were all here in the kitchen."

"Only the three of us, then?"

She nodded. "We had a water fight. You poured a glass of water on my head." She watched him, wondering what his reaction would be.

Garrick took a slow deep breath and let it out. "I remember that," he said. He sounded relieved

"So do I." She grinned like an idiot. It felt so good

to have had a memory that she wrapped her arms around Garrick's neck and kissed him.

After a pause he kissed her back, his tongue stroking hers, his fingers tangling in her hair. The same sensations she'd felt in her memory cascaded through her again. Only this time she knew exactly what they were.

She kissed him until she couldn't stand it anymore, then broke off, breathing hard. Garrick's eyes had a dazed look to them, as if her passion had caught him by surprise.

She stared at his face, noting the differences wrought by time. His jaw was firmer, his cheekbones more sharply defined. His gray eyes seemed deeper than they'd been before, the earlier playfulness mixed with wisdom and experience. The Garrick she held in her arms was a man in the prime years of his masculinity, a husband and a father-to-be.

Her husband, she thought with a jolt of pride. *Her* child's father.

She licked her lips, still feeling the imprint of his kiss. Garrick's eyes tracked the movement of her tongue. He looked as if he wanted to kiss her again, but he didn't.

Taking her hand, he led her out of the kitchen, down the hall and into the library. He closed the door behind them. "Tell me everything you remember," he said.

Samantha gave him the details, from Jenny's first mischievous towel snap to Garrick's sudden departure from the room. At first—embarrassed by her adolescent body's reaction——she didn't admit to the desire that had rocketed through her. But then she reminded herself Garrick was her husband. If she couldn't trust him with her secrets, who could she trust?

Blushing, she told him how her body had felt, how confused she'd been by her response to him.

Garrick betrayed no surprise at her confession.

"You knew, didn't you?" She gave a resigned sigh, thinking how the incident must have changed their relationship. "You knew you'd turned me on."

Garrick didn't say anything. His expression looked a little pained.

"I'm surprised we were still friends afterward," she said. "I mean, it must have made you pretty wary to know you could arouse me so easily...." She gave a forced laugh. "Thank goodness I didn't know what I was feeling, or I might have ripped your clothes off right then and there."

"Yes, thank goodness," Garrick agreed through clenched teeth.

Samantha imagined what might have happened if she'd recognized her desire for what it was. As an impetuous teenager, unaware of the grave consequences of her actions, she might not have hesitated to follow Garrick to his bedroom and do her best to seduce him. Which doubtless would have turned him off. But if by some chance it hadn't, she might have been an unwed teenage mother!

The thought amused her, though she knew the reality of it wouldn't be amusing at all. She told Garrick what she'd been thinking.

He didn't laugh. He just said, "You wouldn't have been unwed."

She rested her hand on his chest. "You would have married me when I was sixteen? How sweet."

"Yes, how sweet." He stood up abruptly, then pulled her to her feet. "What would you like to do with the rest of the afternoon? Go shopping? Take in a movie?"

She laughed. "You don't like thinking about impregnating a sixteen-year-old, do you?"

"No," he said. "I definitely do not."

"Good thing it didn't happen, then. As for this afternoon, I'd like to visit my old apartment."

He stopped halfway to the door. "So soon?"

"Yes. I think it might prompt a few more memories. Do you know what, Garrick? This is the first time since I woke up in the hospital that I'm actually confident my memory will return." She linked her arm through his. "Soon I'll be able to remember everything."

"That's great, Sam," Garrick told her. "Just great. I'll get my car keys."

Visiting her apartment wasn't a good idea, Garrick thought as he killed the engine in front of a pretty yellow house across town. It sat on a quiet residential street near the Hawthorne District, a trendy area of offbeat shops, cafés and bookstores.

Surely she would take one look at the place where she'd lived for three years and get her memory back in a single rush. She'd know exactly who she was, and how she'd gotten into this mess, and she would go running off down the street just as fast as her feet would take her. Away from him.

No, he definitely didn't want to be here.

All during the drive over, Samantha had talked about how excited she was to be getting her memory back. And she'd kept shooting him smoldering looks that as much as said, *when I get it back, I'm going to make love with you.*

If only she knew how wrong she was.

"You lived on the second floor," he told her as he helped her from the car.

She stood on the sidewalk, her hopeful gaze running over the structure, a single-family residence long since converted to three apartments. After studying the house for a full minute, she turned and surveyed the tree-lined neighborhood before looking at the house again.

"Remember anything?" he asked.

Samantha shook her head, obviously disappointed. "No, nothing."

He put an arm around her shoulder and drew her close, feeling selfishly relieved she hadn't, yet wanting to give her comfort. He pointed at the flowers bordering the front lawn. "You and Jenny planted those last year. They're daylilies."

She stared at them for a long time. "Why daylilies?"

"I think Hugh recommended them because they're easy to grow." Garrick led her up to the porch, where he produced her key and unlocked one of the front doors. "The place is still yours for another two weeks," he told her, snapping on a light to reveal a steep staircase.

He led the way upstairs to a spacious, airy room. The apartment was simple but well constructed, with good proportions and a lot of light. On the left, through an archway, were the kitchen and eating area. On the right, the bedroom.

Samantha looked around, tapping her chin as she walked slowly through the main room.

"Your couch was over there," Garrick said, indicating a section of the wall. "You had a television across from it, along with a few plants."

He followed her into the dining area and watched while she poked around the kitchen. She opened the refrigerator, looked into her bare cupboards and ran water in the sink.

It felt strange to see her apartment so empty, he thought. He'd only visited a few times, but he could easily remember how it had looked: lived in and comfortable, with piles of magazines and books...a jigsaw puzzle on the dining table...dishes and cups in the glass-fronted kitchen cupboards...vintage posters of forties film stars. She'd put her stamp on the place, but now it was just an empty apartment.

When Samantha wandered into her bedroom, Garrick hung back in the doorway, leaning against the jamb. Even bare, her bedroom reminded him too strongly of the past, of years of impossible, unrequited desire.

Samantha peered out one of the windows.

"You had pale yellow curtains," he said.

"Where was my bed?" she asked, facing him.

He pointed to the corner. "Right there." At least, that was where it had been the one time he'd seen her room. He'd come to take care of her when she'd had a fever, holding cool cloths to her forehead and wanting to climb into bed beside her.

She walked to the spot and turned around, as if trying to see what the view had been from her bed. She opened her mouth to say something, then shut it again.

"What?" he asked her.

She looked up at him, her eyes wide. "Did we...did we ever...?"

Garrick felt his blood pound. Had they ever made love in her bed? She couldn't know how many times he'd dreamed of being with her in her own room, of waking beside her to sunlight streaming through her yellow curtains. "No," he said, knowing his voice came out strained. "We never did."

They left a few minutes later. Samantha was quiet as he helped her into the car, obviously lost in thought.

"You're upset," he said before starting the engine.

"Just discouraged." She smiled wanly at him. "Sorry I'm not better company."

He took her hand in his and gave it a reassuring squeeze. "Everything will be okay, Sam. You'll get your memory back eventually, and we'll move on with our lives."

"But what if I never do? Maybe all I'm going to

get are little flashes of the past, and I'll never be able to put it all together.''

"Then we'll make new memories for you. Together." Garrick gave her hand another squeeze before releasing it. "But I do think your past will come back." He turned the key in the ignition, and the car roared to life.

Even though I wish it never would, he added silently.

Selfish as it was, he didn't want her to remember the truth. That she hadn't loved him. That they'd never made love.

That he wasn't the father of her baby.

Chapter Six

As they drove off, leaving behind her apartment—
an apartment she didn't recognize—Samantha felt a
twinge of despair. It would be so easy, she thought,
to give in to self-pity.

But somehow she knew that wasn't her style, and
when Garrick suggested they stop for a snack and a
stroll by the river, she managed to quell her bad
mood.

Regardless of her amnesia, she had a husband who
cared for her. He anticipated her pregnant body's
needs, such as frequent food and fresh air. He was
strong and solid and sexy as sin, and she was a very
lucky woman.

They crossed the Hawthorne Bridge and parked
near the waterfront, where a wide strip of grass
stretched for several blocks. Garrick took her hand in

his as they walked along. The warm afternoon had brought out the crowds, especially to the small area of shops that marked one end of the park. A diverse range of people strolled back and forth, or sat on the benches overlooking the marina. The idyllic scene made Samantha feel happier, more peaceful.

"You used to love to come here," Garrick volunteered, surprising her.

She glanced at him. A light spring breeze ruffled his hair, and when he smiled, he looked irresistibly handsome. "With you?" she asked.

"With Jenny, mostly." He found a vacant bench for them. "Here, rest a bit. It's a hot day and you've been on your feet a lot. We don't want them to swell."

Samantha complied, noticing again how thoughtful he was.

"I've heard the snack bar over there has great fruit salad," he said. "Care for a cup?"

She nodded and turned her head to track his departure. He made an impressive figure, she thought. Tall and broad, with just the right amount of muscle.

Suddenly her mind flashed back to the previous night—to sharing his bed. She remembered everything she'd felt lying next to him.

Craving.

Need.

Desire.

Her body heated. Obviously her pregnancy was doing strange things to her hormones! At least, she *hoped* it was. She hoped she didn't always have such lascivious thoughts.

Trying to get herself under control, she focused on the snack bar, which stood a dozen yards away. A frazzled young woman worked alone behind the counter, handling the long line of customers as best she could. A large pink sign announced the place carried "the tastiest smoothies in town." It seemed to influence everyone's orders—usually at the last minute—and only worsened the problem.

The blond man in front of Garrick crossed his arms and tapped his foot. Garrick, however, showed no signs of impatience. He did glance over at Samantha a couple times, winking when he caught her watching.

Then the blond man reached the counter. Though Samantha sat too far away to hear the conversation, she gathered the man wasn't shy about expressing his displeasure to the overworked food server—nor was he satisfied with her apologies. He also had some problem with the six smoothies he ordered and finally stormed off without buying a thing.

The woman looked as if she wanted to cry.

Smiling sympathetically, Garrick stepped up to the counter. He murmured something which, miraculously, got her to smile back, and then he purchased all six of the abandoned drinks as well as the cup of fruit salad. He also slipped a handful of bills into her tip jar—which previous customers had ignored.

Samantha felt her chest swell with pride. Not only was her husband understanding and considerate with *her*, but with total strangers, too.

She watched him turn from the snack bar, carrying a tray. He gave the extra smoothies to a couple of men walking a dog and to a little girl and her mother.

Finally he reached Samantha, with just two of the tall plastic cups left on the tray. He handed her one of them, along with the fruit salad.

"Thank you," she said.

"Don't mention it. Anyway, I have an ulterior motive, remember. I want the baby to be healthy and strong." He patted her gently curved stomach.

"Oh, I don't think that's going to be an issue—I'll be lucky if he or she doesn't come out weighing twelve pounds!" She paused. "You were really sweet back there."

Garrick grimaced. "It wasn't her fault the place is understaffed."

"Still." She sampled her drink, which was wonderfully cool and tangy, and added, "A lot of people would have only thought of themselves. You know, they'd have wanted to be served instantly, no matter what."

He stared out over the water, looking uncomfortable.

Samantha leaned closer to him. Was he blushing? He was! Her handsome, heroic husband was embarrassed by her compliments!

She had to smother a grin. How cute, she thought, digging into her fruit salad. He was chivalrous *and* modest. He was probably the type who stopped to help elderly people across the street, too—not that he'd ever admit it!

* * *

When they got home Jenny greeted them at the front door and whisked Samantha off for a few minutes on the patio. She'd taken her second-to-last exam and was excited for the end of the semester.

Samantha told her about her memory of their water fight in the kitchen, though she omitted the details of her physical response to Garrick.

She did try to broach the subject of her crush, though. "Did I make a fool of myself over him?" she asked.

"Over—over Garrick? No, not really... No, I wouldn't say you did."

Samantha groaned. "I did, didn't I? I'm sure I spent the last ten years making cow eyes at him! How mortifying."

Jenny leaned back on her patio chair. "You never made cow eyes at Garrick."

"Then what *did* I do?"

"Not much, Sam. I wouldn't worry about it. It's all ancient history." Jenny shrugged. "My main concern is the present. How are things going with Garrick? Are you getting, er...reacquainted?"

"Yes, pretty much."

"Pretty much, eh? Not completely? Then I take it you haven't...?"

Samantha swallowed, embarrassed. How could Jenny ask such a personal question? And without even batting an eyelash!

Jenny read the answer in her expression. "Right,

you haven't. Did he give you some line about looking out for your best interests?''

She blinked. "How did you know?''

"Oh, that's just vintage Garrick. He's got a totally overblown sense of honor. He's always trying to put other people's needs before his own.''

Samantha nodded, thinking of their stop by the waterfront. She found something very appealing about such a big, strong man being so kind and thoughtful. "I know, but it's one of the things I like about him. He can be really sweet.''

"True—but don't let him hear you say that!'' Jenny grinned. "He likes to cultivate his gruff and tough exterior.''

They shared a few more minutes on the patio, enjoying the late-afternoon sunshine, before Jenny went to prepare for her last exam.

Samantha wandered to Garrick's study. She found him on the phone, massaging his neck with one hand as he talked. His dark hair stood slightly on end, as if he'd run his fingers through it several times. He looked rumpled and unutterably sexy.

Garrick caught sight of her. The corners of his eyes crinkled when he smiled, and his pleasure was obvious. Samantha's stomach dipped in response.

He waved her into the study, indicating he'd only be a few more minutes. Too restless to sit down, she wandered aimlessly through the room, tuning out his business conversation but not the cadence of his deep, rich voice.

She touched random objects, regarded them without really seeing them. A Mont Blanc fountain pen. A framed award from the mayor on the wall. A blue silk tie tossed onto the file cabinet, one end draped over the edge.

Finally, unable to focus on anything besides her husband, Samantha came to stand behind his chair. Tentatively she placed her hands on the firm neck and shoulder muscles he'd massaged earlier, taking up the task.

She thought about the hours they'd shared since she'd left the hospital. In just a day and half they'd grown more comfortable with each other. And, though their afternoon excursion hadn't generated any more memories, it had definitely made her feel closer to her husband—and more attracted. His behavior at the waterfront had only increased his sexiness.

She pressed her fingers into Garrick's warm skin. If only she could reclaim the past. She wanted to be his wife again—in every sense of the word.

She wanted to explore the contours of his body, to know every inch of it, just as she had before.

"Sam?"

She jerked herself back to reality.

Garrick held the phone away from his face, his palm over the mouthpiece.

"Yes?" she said.

He tilted his head up to give her a wry smile. "That feels great, but could you be a little more gentle?"

Samantha glanced down at her hands, startled to see her thumbs digging deeply into his shoulders, her fingers curled into his chest. "Sorry," she said, forcing her grip to loosen. She stroked his shoulders and lightly kneaded the length of his neck. "Is that better?"

He allowed his head to drop forward, giving her fuller access. "Much."

She stared at his tanned skin above the white collar of his shirt, mesmerized. She loved the feel of him, wanted to indulge in another dreamy moment of sensual imagination.

Could he feel her thoughts? she wondered. Did her fingertips communicate their need to caress every bit of his gorgeous body?

She worked on his neck for several seconds, then noticed he still held the telephone receiver. "Don't you need to finish your conversation?"

His head snapped up. "Damn." He uncovered the mouthpiece and muttered, "I'll get back to you," before dropping the phone into its cradle.

Samantha massaged a while longer, then gave his muscles one last squeeze. She started to pull away, but he raised his hands and laid them over hers, trapping them against his shoulders.

She froze, absorbing the heat of his touch. Neither of them spoke. Neither acknowledged the physical awareness between them.

Then, catching her by surprise, Garrick released her hands. He swiveled his chair and pulled her toward him, turning her hips until she fell neatly onto his lap. He drew her close against his chest. "How was your talk with my sister?" he murmured, his warm breath caressing her ear.

Little electric shivers worked their way through her body, but she strove for a normal tone of voice. "It was fine."

"Did she say anything outrageous?"

"Not really... Nothing too bad."

He traced her jawline with a single finger.

Her skin tingled in its wake.

"You're sure...?"

She nodded, momentarily overwhelmed by sensation. Without thinking, she tangled a hand in his dark, tousled hair. "I—I still think it's strange I can't remember my best friend."

His arms tightened around her, then slowly relaxed. He nudged her a few inches away so he could look into her eyes. "Or your husband."

"That, too." Samantha hardly knew what she was saying. What was happening to her? She gulped for air, feeling his large hands spanning her ribs, seeing the desire in his gaze.

He held her there on his lap, not moving, not kissing her, as if he couldn't help showing how much he wanted her, but wouldn't let himself do anything about it, either.

She remembered his words from the night before. *I want to make love to you. I want to slip inside you and bring us both the relief we deserve.*

And she flushed.

She remembered her own response. *You can make love to me if you want to.*

And she realized how it must have sounded—as if

she were only suffering his attentions for the sake of their marriage, only fulfilling her wifely duties.

Nothing could be further from the truth. She wanted him, every bit as much as he wanted her.

Which was why she couldn't help kissing him.

It was light at first, just on the corner of his mouth. But then she inhaled the heady scent of his skin and felt herself losing control. She parted her lips and touched him with her tongue.

He gave a tortured groan. Very slowly he began to kiss her in return, cupping her nape with one hand, holding her at just the right angle. His other hand still curved possessively around her ribs, squeezing and releasing in the most hypnotic rhythm. Her perceptions seemed to shift sideways, as if she'd slid into a dream.

Garrick trailed his lips to the sensitive spot behind her ear. Tilting her chin up, he pressed moist kisses to her throat. His tongue teased her skin, skimmed over her pulse.

"We should stop," he whispered.

Samantha didn't want to stop. "All right." She undid the top button of his shirt and ran her fingertips along his collarbone.

"It's too soon, Sam." His hand roamed higher on her ribs, brushing the side of her breast.

She tried to suppress a moan. "I know." Her voice came out raspy and thick. Illicit expectation made her insides go shaky.

"This shouldn't...this shouldn't be happening." His thumb grazed the tip of her breast through her lace bra and shirt, and Samantha thought she would die. The caress sent ripples of pleasure through her, pleasure she'd never imagined.

How could she possibly have forgotten this? How could she have shared something so intense with her husband and not remember it?

Groaning again, as if unable to stop, Garrick caressed her through the material. She felt herself tighten with excitement, her body reaching toward him, pressing into his hand.

Their gazes met. Samantha wanted more—she wanted him to slip underneath her shirt, unfasten her bra, touch her without any barriers. And she knew he wanted to, as well. He couldn't look at her like that, his beautiful gray eyes all dark with hunger, if he didn't feel the same.

But he didn't go further. That misguided sense of honor must have kicked in, because he stilled and then slowly lowered his hand. Something flickered in his eyes—guilt?—and his voice was hoarse when he spoke. "I'm sorry, Samantha."

She took a moment to catch her breath. "Don't be. You're my husband."

This didn't seem to comfort him.

"It took a lot more than what we were doing just now to get me pregnant," she pointed out.

He eased her off his lap. "That's not what I meant...."

She leaned her hips back against his desk, waiting.

"We shouldn't have been fooling around in here." Garrick motioned to his study. "If we'd gone much further, I would have ended up—'' He stopped, staring out the window at the wide green lawn.

Ended up making love to me? she thought. Would that have been so terrible?

"You deserve more than a cold desk under your back, Sam."

She knew the words were meant to shock her. They did shock her—with a wave of explicit images that made her toes curl.

He gave a self-mocking laugh. "The damned curtains aren't even closed."

Samantha had the crazy urge to go and draw the curtains. If that was the only problem...

Of course, when she thought about it, Garrick's desk wasn't the most romantic spot to make love. Sure, it might be hot and exciting. But this would be their first time together since she'd gotten amnesia— their first time *ever*, as far as she was concerned. She wanted it to be special.

Samantha regarded her husband. He didn't seem as set against making love as he'd been that morning, she thought. Had he relented? She hoped so.

"Maybe we could..." She trailed off, feeling shy. "Maybe...later...?"

Garrick stared at her for several seconds, long enough for her to regret her words. His eyes were shuttered, unreadable, and she wondered if she'd been too forward.

But then, as if he couldn't help himself, he smiled—a slow, serious, irresistibly attractive smile. "All right, Sam. Later."

* * *

Later.

Just what, exactly, did it mean? Later that night? Or later that year? Had it been a promise or a put off? Samantha wasn't quite sure.

As she and Garrick joined the others in the family room for predinner drinks, she felt restless and edgy. She couldn't stand the suspense of not knowing.

After pouring the sherry—and a ginger ale for Samantha—Garrick sat beside her on the couch. He draped his right arm over her shoulder and proceeded to chat with his mother, tease his sister and generally behave like the charming man he was. All the while, however, his hand toyed with a lock of her hair, twining it around his index finger and, every so often, brushing the bare skin of her neck.

Samantha tried to follow the conversation around her, but Garrick's nearness made that impossible. His body felt hot against hers, and her breathing grew quick and shallow. His touch was intimate and innocent at the same time, as if they'd been married for years. As if, she thought, contact between their bodies was as normal as eating and breathing and sleeping....

She blinked, suddenly realizing the room had gone quiet. She glanced around, trying to recall the topic of conversation, but her mind drew a blank.

Jenny watched her, one eyebrow arched inquisitively. "Well, Sam, do you?"

Embarrassment heated her cheeks. She'd been so absorbed in her response to Garrick that she hadn't heard the question. She took a cooling sip of ginger ale. "Do I what?"

She caught a shared look between Jenny and Beth—a brief curl at the corners of Beth's mouth and an answering grin from Jenny—before Jenny said, "Mom asked if you have anything to wear for that play you and Garrick are seeing this weekend. If not, we can go shopping."

"I—I don't know. I didn't look at my clothes that carefully." She glanced at Garrick. "Do I?"

His fingertips stroked the side of her neck, making her mind go hazy again. "Probably," he murmured, "but it sounds as if Jenny wants to go shopping, so I'd advise you to comply."

"Garrick!" Jenny rolled her eyes and then asked Samantha, "How about Friday morning?"

Garrick traced tiny circles on the skin behind her earlobe. She couldn't focus on the question Jenny had just asked her, so she nodded her head, not caring what she'd agreed to.

She had to get away from her husband, Samantha realized. It was too embarrassing to have him distract her so much she couldn't carry on a simple conversation. She drained her glass and rose to her feet on the pretext of refilling it.

With every step her alertness increased, though she still felt Garrick's magnetic pull. She poured herself another glass of ginger ale from the tray of drinks, sensing his gaze on her the whole time. Knowing he watched her was almost as distracting as being touched by him.

In desperation she circled outside his line of vision. She stopped at the table where last night's jigsaw puzzle lay unfinished, slipping a few more pieces into place before moving on.

Samantha took a closer look around the family room than she had the night before. She read the spines of books on a built-in shelf, and examined the objets d'art and family photos on a sideboard.

It was as she did this that one of the photos caught her eye. Set farther back than the others, the dusty frame was partially obscured by a vase of white flowers.

She reached for it, unsure why it had grabbed her attention. Her stomach tightened, and she wondered if the picture would trigger a memory.

Feeling inexplicably nervous, she blew off the dust and stared at the photo. It showed a group of four, lined up in front of a gaily decorated Christmas tree. She and Jenny—both about seventeen—stood in the middle. Garrick had his arm around Jenny, his smile broad but looking a little forced. On the other side, Samantha clung to a dark-haired young man, her gaze fixed on his handsome face.

She wore an attentive, interested expression, as if she expected him to turn and smile and say just the right words to make her laugh out loud. She looked as if she thought he was the most witty, fascinating person in the world.

Samantha didn't remember who he was, but he looked so much like Garrick he could have been his brother. She stared long and hard at the snapshot, knowing she should recognize the man. But she couldn't summon even the vaguest sense of familiarity. He resembled Garrick so much, yet he didn't spark any of the same feelings Garrick did. He left her feeling cold and unattracted, while the image of Garrick made her remember how it had felt to kiss him, to have his arms around her.

Samantha's anxiety grew. From her body language in the picture, she could tell she knew the man well. And he was obviously a member of the Randall family....

She glanced up from the photo to find Jenny staring at her, eyes wide. Immediately Jenny wiped her features clear, but not before Samantha had seen the look of horror on her face. She wondered what could be so terrible about the picture.

Her mind spun as she tried to come up with an explanation.

Beth and Garrick fell silent, obviously picking up on the abrupt change of energy in the room. Samantha gulped as they turned their heads toward her, feeling oddly unnerved, as if she'd been caught with her hand in the cookie jar.

She took an uncertain step forward, holding out the photo. "Who...who's this?"

Chapter Seven

She'd found the picture of Warren.

Garrick stared at the small wooden frame in Samantha's hand. He recognized it only too well. In the early years he'd picked it up often enough. In order to torture himself. Or to keep from doing anything foolish, like revealing his feelings.

His gut clenched. And now his forgetful wife had found the damned thing.

Would it bring back her memory?

Garrick searched her face, but saw only confusion as she waited for the answer to her question.

Who's this? she'd asked. And someone would have to tell her.

He glanced at his mother and sister, who both watched in silence. "That," he said quietly, "is Warren."

"Warren?"

He clamped his mouth shut. A few sarcastic, inappropriate responses came to mind, but nothing he could say to Samantha. Nothing he would dream of saying aloud—let alone in female company.

Beth, ever the graceful diplomat, picked up the slack. "Warren was my eldest son, Samantha. Jenny and Garrick's brother."

"Oh." She took a moment to assimilate the news, though he could tell it didn't shock her. The family resemblance was difficult to miss. "You used the past tense...."

His mother nodded. "Yes. He died in a boating accident." To Garrick's grim relief, she didn't reveal just how recently that had occurred.

"How awful." Samantha seemed about to add more when Hugh appeared in the doorway to announce dinner.

Jenny leapt to her feet. "Oh, good—I'm famished." With one hand on Beth and the other on Hugh, she bustled them off down the hall.

Garrick went over to Samantha, watching as she carefully replaced the photo on the sideboard.

She still appeared dazed. "I should remember him," she murmured.

"Yes. And undoubtedly you will. Eventually." He tried to keep his voice neutral, though he didn't want her to remember Warren—not now, not when she finally seemed to feel something for *him.*

"He died in a boating accident...."

Reluctantly he nodded. "On vacation in Australia. He'd been drinking."

"Oh, that's terrible. I'm so sorry, Garrick." She touched his arm, her brown eyes wide with sympathy.

Sympathy he didn't need. Didn't deserve. Of everyone in the family, he'd been the one to grieve the least. Hell, sometimes he was *glad* Warren had died. It had given him everything he'd ever wanted.

Garrick felt a stab of guilt at the bitterness he couldn't overcome. The burning resentment. Warren was dead, but he still hadn't managed to forgive him.

He met his wife's gaze. "You're very sweet, Sam. Thank you." He tucked a strand of her long blond hair behind her ear. His thumb brushed her cheek. "We shouldn't keep the others waiting." He drew her close and gave her a reassuring squeeze, then guided her from the room.

She paused in the hall and stared up at him. "I want my memory back, Garrick."

"I know you do."

"It's just so disturbing." She swallowed. "I knew your brother before he died, right? But I look at his picture and...nothing. It's as if he never existed."

Oh, he'd existed, Garrick thought. He'd definitely existed.

If he hadn't, then Samantha—sweet, adorable Samantha—wouldn't be carrying his child.

During dinner, she thought about her discovery. Garrick and Jenny had had a brother. A brother no one wanted to discuss.

Not once during the four-course meal did anyone refer to the photo she'd found. They kept up a steady stream of conversation, but Samantha sensed the underlying tension. The eldest Randall sibling was still on everyone's minds.

She felt bad for reviving their pain. Clearly they hadn't completely gotten over Warren's death.

Washing her face at bedtime, she wondered how *she* had felt about it.

Probably much the same. From everything she'd learned, she'd been like a member of the family for quite some time. She too must have felt as if she'd lost a brother.

Samantha patted her face with a towel. She recalled her anxiety when she'd first seen the picture. For just a moment she'd had a twinge of guilt—as if she'd done something wrong.

She frowned as her head began to hurt. Now what had that guilt been about?

Well, she told herself, probably some part of her had known Warren was dead, despite her amnesia. She must have known she would stir up everyone's grief by reminding them of him.

Pressing a hand to her temple as the headache intensified, Samantha opened the medicine cabinet. She retrieved the painkillers Dr. Hernandez had sent home with her and downed a full dosage.

The pounding made it impossible to think, and she crawled into bed a minute later, moving gingerly so as not to jar her head.

Garrick watched her with concern in his expression. "You okay?" he asked her. "You look wiped out."

She lay back between the cool sheets. "My head started hurting again."

"Just where you bumped it, or all over?" His gaze scanned her face and head.

"Pretty much all over. I took a painkiller." She gave a halfhearted grimace.

Garrick shifted closer. She felt him press a light kiss to her brow. "Anything I can do?"

She shook her head, moving it only a fraction of an inch in either direction. "Actually, if you could turn out the lights…"

He leaned across her to reach the lamp on her bedside table, and she breathed in the scent of his skin. Despite her automatic response to his nearness, she had no thought of continuing what they'd started in his office that day.

Later would have to be some other time. Aside from the fact that she had a headache, she didn't want to make love right after finding the photo—when thoughts of Warren might keep them from concentrating solely on each other.

Garrick seemed to understand that. He turned off the other lamp, leaving the room in darkness. "Well, wake me up if you need anything."

"All right."

He tugged the sheets into place, and then his hand found hers beneath the covers. He laced their fingers together, palm against palm.

They lay in silence. Every few minutes Garrick

shifted on his side of the bed, just as he had the night before. Samantha couldn't get comfortable, either, but confined her restlessness to tiny movements.

Finally Garrick cleared his throat and asked, "How's your headache?"

"Better," she answered. "The painkiller seems to be working."

Another minute passed. Then Garrick gave a ragged sigh, releasing her hand and rolling toward her. "Good. Turn onto your side."

"What?"

One of his hands brushed her thigh, then settled on her hip. "Turn onto your side," he repeated.

"Why?" Her voice came out breathy.

He sighed, sounding annoyed with himself. "Because I won't be able to sleep unless I'm holding you."

At his gruff confession, her hesitance evaporated. Obeying the gentle pressure of his hand, she rolled so her back was to him.

Garrick pulled her close, curling his body around hers, spoon fashion. The soft fabric of his pajama bottoms caressed her bare calves below the hem of her gown.

He spread her hair above her on the pillow, kissed the exposed skin at the back of her neck and cupped a hand protectively around her abdomen. She felt a sensual awareness at having the length of his body pressed against hers, but also a drowsy warmth that pervaded her entire being. She fell asleep almost immediately.

* * *

Garrick slept better than he had in days. Months, really, if he wanted to be exact. Holding his wife all night long was like nothing he'd ever experienced.

It seemed to help Samantha as well. In the morning she looked well rested and assured him her headache had dissipated. She felt energetic enough to visit a baby boutique his mother had mentioned the previous evening.

They drove to the shop after breakfast. Located in an old Victorian house, the place carried a vast assortment of clothes, supplies and educational toys.

Samantha grinned as they worked their way through the store, laughing every time he put an item in their shopping basket. For each one that she allowed to remain, she returned four or five to their displays.

"Garrick," she chastised him at one point. "These pajamas are sized for a two-year-old. Don't you think you're jumping the gun?"

He shrugged as she replaced them on the rack. "She's going to need them eventually."

Samantha shook her head. "Right. If I'd let you, you'd buy the whole store.... Hey, how do you know it's a she?"

"I don't. I just thought a girl would look cuter in PJs with little blue cars on them. You know, to avoid sex-role stereotyping."

She rolled her eyes. "Ooookay. Look, if you really want to check out Pjs, we should go back to the newborn section."

"Oh, no. That's all right. I'd rather look at those."
He pointed to a wall of miniature neon-framed sunglasses. "Wouldn't Junior look hip in them?"

"Just what I want," she said, trailing after him. "A hipster baby."

She came to stand by his side. While he made a show of inspecting the styles—just to tease her—she leaned against him and rested a hand at his waist.

Catching sight of himself and Samantha in one of the shop's mirrors, Garrick felt his heart quicken. They looked like such a...such a couple. Happy. As if they loved each other, loved being together.

He felt her warmth against his side through the fabric of his shirt. The urge to turn her in his arms and kiss her almost overwhelmed him. If they hadn't been in public, he would have.

Samantha smiled up at him. "I can't believe Beth bought *your* baby clothes here. That's so cute."

"I think the merchandise has changed since then," he said.

"What, you don't think they sold baby sunglasses thirty years ago?"

"Don't know—but my father would have had a fit if Mom had put anything neon on my little body. His tastes were more conservative."

She chuckled. "Tell me about your father. What was your relationship like?"

Garrick hesitated.

"Go on, you can tell me."

He took a deep breath. He'd hardly discussed the subject with her *before* her amnesia. Hardly discussed it with anyone, really. "I didn't know Dad that well until I went to work for him."

"Why not?"

"When we were little, he always left for the office before we woke up—and came home after we'd gone to sleep. As soon as I turned sixteen, though, I started working at the company each summer vacation—sorting mail, running errands, filing. Sometimes I'd go to lunch with Dad—it was more time than I'd ever spent with him."

Samantha absently tapped her chin. "Do you think that's one reason you were so dedicated to your work?"

"Sure. No doubt."

"And that's why you rose to the top so fast."

Garrick shrugged. "It didn't hurt to be the boss's son, but yes. The more responsibility I had, the closer I got to my father." He paused and met her gaze. "Sam, I plan to be there for you and the baby. You can count on me for that."

"I know I can." She gave him a tender, appreciative look. "Garrick, you're going to be such a wonderful parent."

He hoped so. Despite his feelings about Warren, he already loved the baby to distraction. Just as he loved its mother.

They continued shopping, stopping at a tall display of stuffed animals. A teddy bear caught his eye, and he showed it to Samantha.

"Jenny had one a lot like this," he told her. "Of course, by the time she got through with it, it had only one button eye left and its nose was hanging by a thread. It's probably still in the attic somewhere.''

Samantha took the bear from him, squeezing it a few times to test its softness. She rubbed the fur against her cheek.

"Like to buy it?"

She nodded and dropped it into the basket, saying, "How did I become friends with Jenny?"

He winked at her. "I don't know if I should tell you that."

"Oh, come on." She gave his arm a playful little punch. "What could it hurt? I promise it won't plant a false memory."

Garrick let her wheedle him a bit longer, enjoying the lighthearted interaction, before he relented. "Oh, all right. You ran into each other at a soccer game. Literally. Head to head. You were trying to keep her from scoring the winning goal against your team, and you did so, effectively."

She gaped at him. "Not on purpose?"

"No, you didn't mean to hit her on the head that way, but you were both moving so fast it was unavoidable. At least, that's how my mother told it. She said she heard the impact clear across the field."

"Oh, ouch!"

"You and Jenny made friends on the sidelines, both holding ice packs to your heads. Jenny loves to tell the story." He selected a few baby rattles and tossed them on top of the teddy bear.

Without comment, Samantha returned two of them to their shelf. "So you weren't there?"

"No. I was back east at college."

"What about...Warren?"

The question caught him off guard. They hadn't mentioned Warren since she'd found the photo in the family room. He'd hoped to avoid discussing him indefinitely. "No," he said at last. "He was away at school, too."

By that time his brother had been kicked out of three colleges for partying too much and studying too little, and was only at the fourth by virtue of their father's generous gifts to the annual fund.

Samantha frowned. "Did I know him very well?" she asked softly.

What could he say to that? The answer was more complex than yes or no, but he didn't want to give away too much. "I don't think any of us knew him well. He was hardly ever home."

"But he lived at the house with the rest of you?"

Garrick shook his head. "Not really. Warren liked to travel. He spent most of his time at condos and resorts."

Her eyebrows shot up. "Didn't that get expensive?"

"Sure. But he had a trust fund, as well as a substantial interest in the company."

"Oh. Right..." She let a few seconds pass. "Did he die a long time ago?"

Garrick stared down at her face. She'd asked the question gently, as if she thought it would hurt him. Ironically, Warren's death had caused her ten times more pain that it had ever caused him. "No, but we've tried to put it behind us."

"Is that why there aren't many pictures of him in the house? Why you never talk about him?"

"Yes, in a way. There's really not that much to say."

Something in his tone must have hinted at his feelings, because Samantha studied his face for a long moment before speaking. "You didn't get along, did you?"

He couldn't bring himself to lie. "Maybe when we were very young. We were very different people, Sam. We tolerated each other, but there was no way we would have been close. We hardly ever saw eye-to-eye."

Which was putting it mildly. Warren had been a selfish bastard, manipulative and unscrupulous. Unworthy of Samantha's love. Incapable of returning her affection, or of giving her the care she deserved.

Garrick put the brakes on his unpleasant thoughts. To get angry about the past would do none of them any good. He should just be grateful things had worked out as they had. After all, he and Samantha were married now, and they had a baby to love and raise together.

Even if it had all come about the wrong way, they might be able to make it right.

They walked together to the counter, their shopping spree winding down.

"What about Warren and Jenny?" she asked.

"They got on a little better." That was all he wanted to say. He'd already said way too much.

She seemed to accept his answer. "I guess I'll understand it more if and when I get my memory back."

"Probably." He just hoped she fell in love with him first.

They got in line behind an African-American couple with a newborn infant. He and Samantha both watched the baby, then looked at each other and smiled.

Garrick felt his chest tighten. He still couldn't believe that in six short months they'd have one of their own. Suddenly it struck him as miraculous.

Watching her husband, Samantha knew he felt the same sense of wonder she did. She flushed, feeling closer to him than she ever had before.

Back in the car she asked him what he knew of her childhood.

"You were happy," he said, pulling into the street. "Well loved. But it's all secondhand, Sam. Just little things you told me, or things I picked up from Jenny."

"Like what?"

"Your parents used to rent a cabin on the coast for a week every summer. I've seen snapshots of you as a child on the beach, in a little blue swimsuit with your toes in the water and a look of absolute glee on your face."

"I'd like to see that." She wondered if she still had the pictures somewhere.

He described her parents, who'd died separately

within a few months of each other. They'd been fairly old when they'd had her. He told her she had a photo of them on her desk at the office.

Garrick also talked about her school activities. "In addition to soccer and community service, you always wrote for the paper. I remember you used to conduct a lot of polls."

"Training for my job in marketing, I bet."

He grinned and nodded.

It was so strange, she reflected, that he knew more about her past than she did—at least for the moment. She was glad he'd told her more details today.

But she couldn't help wishing, for the hundredth time, that she could remember them herself.

They arrived home to another delicious meal cooked by Hugh. After lunch she took a nap, then asked Garrick to show her the attic. He'd told her she'd placed some items in storage there, and she wanted to look through them.

The attic was hot and slightly stuffy. After cracking open a window, Garrick removed the dustcovers from her things. He revealed a farmhouse-style dining table, four simple matching chairs, a few lamps, a bureau, and an armchair upholstered in lime green polyester with tiny purple flowers.

She stared at the chair. "It's hideous!" she exclaimed.

Garrick nodded. "But comfortable, you always said. I got the impression you were very fond of the thing.... It doesn't bring up any memories?"

No memories—just the feeling that perhaps her taste was not as good as she would have preferred. She ran her hand across the fabric. "I really liked this?"

"Try sitting on it," Garrick suggested.

She did so, gingerly.

The chair was deceptively comfortable. It cradled her body perfectly. It was the kind of chair on which to spend long hours, she thought, reading a book or staring out the window.

And then, as she sat there—and much to her surprise—a memory did come.

Chapter Eight

Samantha's mind flashed back to a cool fall day in the not-too-distant past. She could feel the fresh air in her lungs, see the orange and red colors of the trees and the newly fallen leaves scattered across the yards in her neighborhood.

She and Garrick had been combing tag sales near her apartment when she'd spotted the chair. She'd tried it out as a joke, knowing she would never actually own anything so ugly, but had been amazed by how good it felt to sit on. She'd had to borrow ten dollars from Garrick to come up with the cash to buy it.

Samantha grinned up at her husband, thinking of what he'd said when he'd first laid eyes on the chair. "You called it the furniture crime of the century."

He stared at her. "Did you just—did you just remember that?"

"Yes," she said, still grinning. "We bought it together, right?"

Garrick didn't answer at first, as if making a mental adjustment. Then he smiled almost reluctantly. "Over my protests, as I recall."

"But I talked you into it," she returned, amazed how good it felt to have another memory. "You carried it home on your head."

She smiled, remembering how she'd teased Garrick mercilessly on the way home, poking fun at how he looked with her ugly chair on his head.

A block from her apartment, a small terrier out for its afternoon walk had started barking madly at him, no doubt thinking he was a space alien come to invade the peaceful neighborhood. The woman on the other end of the terrier's leash had given Garrick a strange look, echoing her dog's confusion.

Samantha had whispered to the woman, "He's color-blind. He can't tell how ugly it is," just loudly enough for Garrick to hear. He'd swung around to scowl at her, his face framed by the arm of the chair. Although his expression had been fierce, his eyes had sparkled with amusement. She'd giggled, causing the woman and her terrier to go off in a huff.

Samantha probed the rest of her memory, trying to find its boundaries. In total, she recalled about an hour. And everything about it indicated a close and caring relationship between herself and Garrick.

She'd felt completely at ease in his presence. The mood between them had shifted from lively banter at the tag sale to relaxed intimacy in her apartment as she sat on her new chair and watched him make a pot of coffee.

She was going to get her memory back, she thought with renewed confidence. Her amnesia wouldn't last forever. She wouldn't have to go through the rest of her life with a great blank page where twenty-five years of memories should be. They would come back, slowly but surely.

And if all of them were like this one, with herself and Garrick being so happy together...

Of course, this memory didn't include the same intense physical desire as yesterday's. But it must have been there all the same. Over the years she would have learned to hide her attraction from Garrick—and from herself, too, so she could enjoy his friendship without unrequited feelings getting in the way.

Thank goodness she didn't have to hide her attraction from him anymore, she thought.

They examined the rest of her belongings—without further incident—before heading back downstairs. While Garrick worked in his study, Samantha sat in the breakfast room, enjoying a tall mug of steamed milk.

Hugh kept her company, tending his ferns while she told him about her recent memory.

"The only thing I don't understand," she said, "is why I remember some things and not others." She stared down into her mug. "It frustrates me sometimes. I guess I just wish it would all come back at once, instead of in bits and pieces.''

Hugh joined her at the table. "I can understand. Memory loss is very unsettling.'' He put one of his big hands on hers. "I've never told you this, but before Beth found me and got me dried out, I was drinking so heavily I'd have blackouts. There's still a whole week of my life I can't remember at all.''

"Oh, Hugh, how awful!''

He shrugged. "From what people tell me, I wouldn't want to remember that week even if I could—sometimes it's best just to leave things behind.''

Hugh had a point, she thought. So far she'd had only good memories, but she knew life wasn't that perfect. There might be things in her past she'd be better off not knowing about.

A sudden chill made her shiver. She took another sip of hot milk, telling herself it meant nothing. Even if she'd had her share of ups and downs, nothing could be *that* terrible. Nothing could change the fact that she had a wonderful husband and carried his child and felt so close to his family.

She and Hugh discussed her amnesia some more, and he asked about her other memory. She described the water fight, giving him the same chaste version she'd told to Jenny.

Frowning thoughtfully, Hugh returned to his plants and misted them in silence. Then he stopped and stared out the window a moment, eyes narrowed.

Samantha watched him curiously. "What is it?" she said. "What are you thinking?"

Slowly he turned to face her. "That your two clearest memories were set off by sensory triggers—by feeling or touching something."

She stared at him. "Why, you're right."

The first time she'd had her hand on Garrick's steam-dampened shirt, and the second time she'd sat on the unexpectedly comfortable chair.

A grin stole over her face. "They don't come when I just look at something, like my apartment or a photo, but when I can actually feel something." She paused, thinking of how many things she'd touched in the past few days. Only two of them had sparked memories. "Well, sometimes they do," she admitted.

"Maybe it's only when you've done the same thing before."

"Right..." She considered what that could mean. The two memories had occurred when she'd repeated things she'd done with Garrick.

If she repeated more things she'd done with him, her memory might come back faster. Sure, she wouldn't get a memory every time, but she might get enough to piece together most of her past.

She was still mulling it over when Hugh left to start dinner and Jenny arrived home and invited her outside.

The two women strolled through the gardens.

"All right, what is it?" Jenny said almost immediately. "What's on your mind? Did something happen?"

Samantha told her about Hugh's brainstorm, and her idea to catalyze more memories.

"Oooh, how interesting..." She smiled, then sobered. "But why the big rush to get it all back? Whether you do or not, it shouldn't change your situation much. Especially not with my brother. I mean, you married him for forever, Sam. I was there at the wedding. I heard the 'till death do you part' stuff. You're stuck with him, so you might as well get on with loving the guy."

Samantha grimaced. "I just wish I could remember loving him before."

Jenny was silent for several paces, her expression curiously blank. Finally she said, "Love isn't something you need to remember, Sam. Love is something you feel right now. Memory or not."

They walked for a few more minutes before Jenny had to return to her studies. Samantha remained outside, sitting on the bench that overlooked the city below.

She felt torn. Part of her wanted to do what Jenny advised—stop worrying about the past and just live in the moment. But another part of her couldn't stand not knowing exactly how things had been. Not knowing exactly what she'd thought and felt before her accident. That was one thing nobody else could tell her.

Samantha sighed, knowing she wouldn't stop trying to get her memory back. She had to test her idea, had to repeat her past experiences with Garrick and see what happened.

The only tricky part, she thought, would be to figure out what things she'd done with him before. She didn't relish a lifetime of hit-and-miss attempts to repeat her actions.

It wasn't until later, as she sorted through the purchases she and Garrick had made at the baby boutique, that the realization came to her.

She was pregnant—which meant there was at least one event in her past she could isolate with absolute certainty.

She'd made love with her husband.

That had to be one of the most intense physical experiences a person could have. Thinking of Garrick, of his sexy male body and her powerful attraction to him, she could easily convince herself that making love would help her reclaim the past.

Surely if anything could spark a memory, it was that. Surely if she repeated such a sensual act, knew Garrick on such an intimate level, she'd remember having known him before.

It seemed like a risk worth taking. Either way, she would get to be with her husband.

As bedtime approached, however, Samantha grew nervous. She dawdled in the family room after dinner, working on the jigsaw puzzle, and Garrick had to urge her upstairs. Due to her distraction, she took twice as long as usual to brush her teeth and wash her face.

"Is something wrong?" Garrick asked as she joined him in bed. "You seem pretty tense."

Samantha felt an attack of shyness. She fussed with

the covers, wondering what to do. Just blurt out her idea and proposition him?

Not appealing. Though it might work, it was just too unromantic.

Garrick leaned toward her, tipping up her chin with his finger. "Has something upset you?"

She shook her head. "No, I was just…just wondering…" *Just wondering if maybe you'd like to make love to me.*

"Yes?" He lowered his hand to hers, squeezing it.

His hands, she thought, were gentle and strong and sexy. Just like the rest of him. She couldn't help wanting to feel those hands span her ribs again, have him touch her as he'd done the day before.

But she couldn't make herself say it. So she asked him for a back rub instead.

Garrick smiled. "I owe you one, don't I? Roll onto your stomach."

Samantha remembered something she'd seen in her nightstand next door. "Wait," she said, "I'll be right back."

She returned with the bottle of massage oil and placed it in his hand. He stared at it as she climbed back in bed.

She lay down on her stomach and waited.

Garrick didn't move.

Several seconds ticked by.

Suddenly she realized the problem. He couldn't apply the oil through her nightgown. "Oh, sorry," she mumbled, blushing. Keeping her front on the bed and the covers above her waist, she tugged the hem up to her neck.

Nothing happened.

"Garrick?" She glanced over her shoulder.

He hadn't even opened the bottle. He stared down at her bare back. "Are you trying to seduce me, Sam?"

She parted her lips, then closed them again. She *hadn't* been trying to seduce him. Well, not consciously, anyway. "I...I'm not sure," she confessed, embarrassed.

Garrick cleared his throat. "Let's just start with the massage."

Samantha heard him flick up the cap. He poured oil onto his hand, then rubbed his palms together to warm it.

She closed her eyes. Her senses felt amplified. Every rustle seemed loud in her ears. The subtle scent of the massage oil drifted to her nose, and her skin tingled in anticipation.

Finally Garrick's hands touched her shoulder blades. She told herself to stay relaxed, though her whole body snapped to attention.

He swept downward along her spine, then feathered back up over her ribs, distributing the oil. The smooth, repetitive motion lulled her into a trancelike state. Sighing, she sank into the mattress.

Garrick kneaded her shoulder muscles with strong, capable fingers. He paid special attention to the tops of her arms and, after working slowly down her body once more, pressed deeply into the small of her back, banishing the last traces of tension.

Samantha thought she'd gone to heaven.

He finished with another round of wide, circular strokes before easing her nightgown back down.

She gave a little moan of satisfaction. "That felt wonderful," she murmured, so languid she could barely form the words.

"I'm not finished yet." He pulled her nightgown only far enough to cover her bottom, then removed the bedclothes from her legs.

"Garrick...?"

"Get used to it, Sam," he said gently. "When you start having leg cramps, massages like this will be part of our daily routine."

Samantha didn't know what he meant until she remembered that leg cramps, like tiredness and morning sickness, often accompanied pregnancy. But, she thought, since she hadn't been sick, maybe she wouldn't have leg cramps, either.

Before she could say anything, Garrick had warmed more oil between his palms and started on her legs.

It felt too good to resist. He thoroughly massaged each of her calves, then moved higher. He worked on both thighs at once, skimming up to just below the curve of her bottom before sliding back down.

At first he didn't go near the insides of her thighs, but then he did, working slow, deliberate magic with his hands. He advanced gradually upward, thoroughly relaxing each stretch of muscle before moving on.

She no longer knew who was seducing whom. Garrick's touch wasn't overtly sexual—it felt almost detached, as if he were a professional masseur performing his duties without crossing the line—but nevertheless it aroused her. She didn't know where his hands would stop, how high they would climb before he ended the delicious torture and swept back downward.

Finally his hands did stop, well before the point where a massage ended and something else began. He tugged the nightgown safely to her knees, stretched his long frame beside her and pulled up the covers.

Samantha tried to normalize her breathing. She lay with her head turned away from him, flustered by her response—and her foolish imagination. "Thank you," she managed.

"My pleasure." His voice was husky, almost hoarse.

Maybe he'd been more affected than she'd thought. She rolled onto her side to face him.

His position mirrored hers, except for his head, which was propped on one hand. He smiled down at her, then raised a finger to brush a tendril of hair from her cheek. "You're irresistible, Sam."

Without really planning it, she leaned over so her lips were only inches from his throat. Her hand came up and grasped his shoulder for support. She could see the steady beat of his pulse beneath the skin of his neck. "So are you," she whispered.

Tentatively she kissed his throat, tasting his skin, feeling his blood pound. A delightful sense of power rippled through her. Threading her fingers in his hair, she kissed her way up to his jaw. She savored the texture of his five o'clock shadow, liking the way it delicately scraped her lips and cheeks, then traced the curve of his ear with her tongue.

"Do you know what you're doing, Sam...?"

She paused to look up at him. She felt flushed, intoxicated. "Um, no...not really." Her voice, throaty and rough, didn't sound like her own.

"I didn't think so," he said.

But he didn't stop her. He lay still, compliant, while she kissed his cheek, his eyelids and finally his mouth.

Samantha felt an intense, emotional response—as if all her feelings of the past few days had finally found a channel, a means of release.

And the kiss became more than a kiss. It became everything she wasn't brave enough to say out loud.

She nibbled on his lips. I want you, Garrick.

She traced the seam of his mouth. Make love to me. Caress every inch of my skin. Drive me so wild with desire I can't stand it anymore.

She touched her tongue to his, intoxicated by the contact. Garrick, I need you. Now.

She explored his taste and textures as her heart hammered a ragged rhythm. I love you.

The thought shouldn't have shaken her, but it did.

Nothing on earth could be more normal, more absolutely prosaic, than for a wife to love her husband.

But it didn't feel normal. Not at all. She felt out of

control, as if she'd slipped on an icy sidewalk—or her car had spun out on a curvy road.

If she'd loved him for years, loved him enough to sleep with him and to marry him, realizing her feelings shouldn't be an issue. But even if she had, she didn't remember it. The love she felt right now wasn't remembered love at all, but current love.

Love isn't something you need to remember, Sam. Love is something you feel right now. Memory or not...

Kissing her husband, Samantha definitely felt it.

She loved him.

Irrevocably.

Her pulse racing, Samantha pulled away enough to study Garrick's face.

In the light from the bedside lamp, he looked unbearably handsome. His features were masculine and exquisitely sculpted. A lock of dark hair fell over his brow, and his pupils were dilated, nearly concealing the gray irises.

She gave him a tremulous smile. Surely the fact that she'd fallen in love with him all over again was a good sign. It meant the bond between them was strong—strong enough to transcend anything, even amnesia.

She might have woken up in the hospital and come to hate him, or realized she didn't much care for him one way or another. Might have.

But she hadn't.

"Samantha?"

She didn't even try to hold back. Giddy with the

knowledge of her feelings, she wrapped her arms around him. "Garrick," she said, "it's the most amazing thing."

"What is?"

"That I'm madly in love with you." She buried her face in his neck, inhaling his spicy male scent. She knew she would never get enough.

Chapter Nine

Garrick felt as if the air had been sucked from his lungs.

He wondered if he'd lost his hold on reality. He'd been damn close to losing his mind ever since she'd asked for that back rub, but—

Had she just told him she loved him?

"Oh, I haven't gotten my memory back," she said, pressing warm, moist kisses to his throat. "But I didn't need to. I love you right now, even without it—"

Garrick didn't let her finish, just angled her face up to his and kissed her with barely controlled emotion.

He'd loved her so long, wanted her so long, that her words set off an inexorable reaction.

He simply had to have her.

If she'd protested, of course, he would have found

the strength to stop—but he was just as glad he didn't have to do so. Samantha pressed herself willingly against him, returning his passion with her own.

She smelled of rose petals and massage oil, and it drove him crazy. He kissed every bit of her exposed skin, caressed her breasts through the flimsy fabric of her nightgown.

She sighed, and moaned, and whimpered.

He brought his lips to her ear. "You know what's going to happen, don't you?"

"Yes," she said, "I do. Make love to me."

At the honest desire in her voice, Garrick forced himself to pause, to keep his hands motionless. Forced himself not to rip the gown right off her.

She deserved more than a brief, frantic mating of bodies. She deserved all the tender slowness he could give her.

And the waiting would increase her pleasure.

Kissing her throat, he touched her again through the silky material. He stroked the curve of her breast, circling toward its peak and then away again, never quite touching it.

She shifted restlessly.

Garrick unfastened the top button of her nightgown, then skimmed the vee of bare skin with his tongue.

She arched her back to give him better access. "Please, Garrick."

"Easy," he said. He touched the tip of her breast.

Samantha expelled her breath in a rush. Her pleasure almost undid him. He struggled for control as he freed a few more buttons on her gown. With shaking fingers he brushed the sleeves off her shoulders.

He couldn't believe this was real—couldn't believe they were finally together the way he'd always wanted. It felt too good, too perfect.

But then he ceased thinking entirely, lost himself in touching his wife, in her gratifying responses. He teased her breasts with his tongue and mouth until she turned her head from side to side on the pillow, urging him on with her words and with her trembling body. He touched her everywhere, and soon she was touching him, too.

When he knew neither of them could take any more, he stripped them both of their remaining clothes. They lay naked, completely vulnerable to each other.

Garrick reached between them, stroking her. He explored the moist heat of her. "Are you ready?" he asked.

Foolish question. She was more than ready.

But she answered him anyway. "Yes," she said. And she pulled him on top of her.

It was all the encouragement he needed. Raising his hands to cup her face, he kissed her with all the love of the last ten years as he slipped inside her.

The sensations overwhelmed them both. She fit snugly around him, her dampness welcoming his hardness. They lay still for several moments, just drinking in the feel of each other, before he began to move his hips.

Almost immediately her body reached toward release. Deliberately slowing his strokes, he drew out every last fragment of her pleasure.

But nothing could keep her from falling apart in his arms. Her muscles contracted around him, driving them both over the edge. Groaning, Garrick pressed his lips to hers, kissing her once again, swallowing her cries of fulfillment.

He felt like a louse.

A weak, depraved, dishonest louse.

Garrick stared at the ceiling above his bed. His sleeping wife lay in the crook of his arm, snuggled against him like a kitten. The wife he'd finally claimed as his own.

The wife he'd taken under false pretenses.

The cold light of morning made his actions look sleazy. Sure, Samantha had said she loved him—even now, the memory made his heart quicken. But could her love survive the truth? Or would she hate him once she learned?

Garrick wouldn't blame her if she asked for a divorce. He'd had no right to make love to her last night, as wonderful as it had been.

Never mind that he'd been crazy with happiness. Never mind that he'd loved her for ages.

If he'd waited this long to have her, he could have waited just a little bit longer—until she'd gotten her memory back. Eventually she might have learned to love him on her own, without the help of amnesia.

But now she'd have to get past his deception first. She'd have to forgive him. And even a saint would have trouble doing that. He certainly couldn't do it himself.

He should have told her everything as soon as she awoke in the hospital. He should tell her now—wake her up and tell her he'd lied by omission, that their marriage was a sham.

But no, he couldn't tell her. After she'd shared herself with him so intimately, the truth would be devastating. It might, as Jenny had argued, jeopardize her health. He couldn't take that chance. He'd never forgive himself if he caused her to have a miscarriage.

He just hoped Samantha's mind would take care of her, would release her memories slowly enough that she could come to terms with the past without being overwhelmed.

In the meantime he knew no one else would let the truth out, either. Jenny certainly wouldn't, and Beth and Hugh were much too discreet, too tactful. Though they'd never discussed it with him, he knew they'd both known what he felt for Samantha—and what she hadn't felt for him. And he assumed they'd guessed what had happened to bring about their marriage. To anyone who knew the participants, the sordid details weren't difficult to imagine.

He tensed automatically at his thoughts, and Samantha stirred in his arms. She stretched sensually, then opened her eyes.

"'Morning," she said, her voice sleep-soft and husky.

Garrick stared down at her. She looked...satisfied.

Obviously she wasn't having regrets about making love with him. Her smile was too warm, too genuine.

He wanted her again. He wanted to forget the past and the future. Damn, but he wanted her again.

Suppressing his renewed desire, he kissed her on the tip of her nose. "Good morning, Sam. How do you feel?"

"Mmmm." She closed her eyes and relaxed against him, her skin soft and very naked along the length of his body. "Good. Sleepy. But I didn't have a memory."

"Oh?"

She stretched again. "I'd thought I might," she murmured, "because of all the sensations."

"Sensations," he repeated. Was she really awake?

"Yes. I thought if we made love, I might remember doing so before."

He frowned. "Samantha, look at me."

She opened one eye. "What?"

"You thought it would set off a memory?"

"Mmm-hmm. 'Cause it's such a strong sensory trigger." Drowsily she explained her reasoning. "I guess it wasn't that great an idea, though, since it didn't work."

Garrick wasn't so sure. Last night hadn't disproved her theory, but he couldn't exactly tell her why—that she'd never been with him before. "I'm sorry," he said, hating himself for the subterfuge.

Samantha seemed only mildly disappointed. "Oh, well. To tell you the truth, I forgot all about getting my memory back while we were...you know..." She stopped, her cheeks turning pink.

He felt his body respond to her words, to images of last night. Damn, but he was like an adolescent boy around her. "Good," he said, his voice gruff.

"And now that we have..." She paused and bit her lip. "Well, you're not going to go back to saying we can't, are you?"

"No, Sam." Garrick wished he could resist temptation, but he wasn't going to fool himself. One night with his wife would never be enough. It had only made him want her more.

Her amnesia, he thought, was certainly making him see an unsavory side of himself. A side disturbingly similar to his brother. Maybe he and Warren hadn't been as different as he'd always wanted to believe.

Though their lovemaking hadn't brought a memory, Samantha didn't have to wait long before something else did.

That afternoon Jenny sent Garrick out for ice cream while she and Samantha checked her jewelry collection for something to wear to the theater.

They were heading back downstairs when Garrick returned from his errand. They'd almost reached the marble staircase to the entrance hall and could clearly hear his key in the solid brass lock of the front door.

Samantha stopped in her tracks as the tumblers clicked into place and the latch slid back with a snap. Jenny kept going, rushing down to meet her brother. Left behind in the hallway, Samantha felt a jolt of recognition. She knew, with absolute certainty, that a memory was coming. As soon as she turned the corner, the images would fall into place.

She almost didn't do it. A sudden sense of anxiety almost made her turn around and run right back to her room. Which was ridiculous—she wanted her memory back, didn't she?

Forcing herself to continue, Samantha stepped off the padded hall carpet and onto the hard marble stairs. She gripped the handrail tightly and let her gaze drop to the entryway.

Jenny stood with her brother, reaching for the bag of ice cream he held. Samantha saw them, but she saw a different picture as well. The two scenes—one from the present and one from the past—were superimposed on the same background. She saw Jenny in her twenties and also in her teens. She saw Garrick as he was and also as a very young man. And beside that other Garrick she saw a third person, as well.

Warren.

She recognized him at once. He looked a few years younger than he'd been in the photograph, but there was no mistaking his identity.

The two brothers had just come home for the holidays. Samantha remembered she and Jenny had been upstairs, trying out a new computer puzzle, when they'd heard a car in the drive. She remembered Jenny's excitement, how she'd jumped up from her desk and launched herself down the hallway. Samantha, being more reserved, had followed with tentative steps.

She'd never met Jenny's brothers before, and had felt a little nervous. Their laughing voices had carried up to her as she rounded the corner to the stairs. And then she'd looked out across the entrance hall, just as she was doing now.

She'd caught her breath as she saw the best looking guy in the world. Tall and dark, he stood with self-assured elegance. He wore stylish clothes and a charming, utterly dazzling grin.

Samantha was definitely dazzled. She stared in awe for several seconds, no longer hearing her best friend's chatter.

Then the man glanced up with a raised eyebrow. "And who's this?" he said in a smooth-as-silk voice. "She looks like a princess from one of your novels."

From that moment on, he'd been her hero.

The grown-up Jenny intruded on her memory. "Sam? Aren't you coming?"

Samantha focused on her friend. She felt disconnected, confused. Swallowing the tightness in her throat, she managed a nod.

"Well, then, what are you waiting for? The ice cream's melting." Jenny plucked the bag from her brother's hands and took off down the hallway.

Garrick remained, waiting for Samantha to descend the rest of the stairs. She did so, barely aware of her movements, and allowed him to escort her to the breakfast room.

The ice cream might as well have been sawdust. She ate it mechanically, not tasting it. She sat at the table with her husband and best friend, but couldn't have said what they discussed.

Her mind was in the past, dwelling on that flash of girlish attraction she'd felt.

Attraction that hadn't been for Garrick, but for Warren.

When she'd woken up at the hospital, she'd assumed she'd had a crush on Garrick since the moment they'd met. Obviously she'd been wrong. In her memory she was hardly aware of Garrick at all. He was just the guy who stood next to Warren. Sure, Jenny had run to Garrick first, leaping up into his arms for a welcoming hug, but Warren—elegant, charming Warren—had claimed all of Samantha's attention.

Her head started to ache.

Oh, dear Lord, she thought. If she'd been wrong about her crush on Garrick, she was probably wrong about other things, too.

Since coming home from the hospital, she'd constructed a story about her growing love for Garrick— about how her childhood crush had changed into a deeper love, until she'd slept with him, gotten pregnant and married him.

But that was just a story. The first part of it wasn't true; the rest might be a lie, too.

She thought of the odd moments of apprehension she'd experienced. Had she been too quick to discount them?

Thank goodness there wasn't any way to misinterpret her desire for Garrick during the water fight. And the affection between them was clear in her memory of buying the chair.

Even if she'd had a crush on Warren at first, she told herself, that didn't change the way she felt about her husband. She loved him, and he cared for her, as well. Why else would he have stayed all night at the hospital, read all those baby books, been so attentive and comforted her every time she felt overwhelmed? He was a strong, successful, considerate man. He possessed an admirable sense of honor, and he was damned attractive to boot!

Her attraction to Warren must have faded fast. A few weeks, or maybe a year at the most, and she would have realized that Garrick was the real man of her dreams.

Samantha stopped herself. She sounded desperate, as if she was trying too hard to convince herself.

If everything was fine, then why had that memory of Warren upset her so much? And even though she and Garrick seemed to have the perfect relationship, hadn't he told her they'd been fighting right before her accident?

She sighed in frustration, wishing she could just live her life instead of analyzing it so much. Jenny was probably right. The past didn't matter.

"Anything wrong, Sam?"

She looked up to find both Garrick and Jenny staring at her with concerned expressions. She dragged herself away from her morbid thoughts and attempted a smile. "Sorry, I was just—" she searched for a suitable half-truth "—just wallowing in self-pity."

Jenny grinned brightly. "Mood swings are part of being pregnant. Have some more ice cream."

She shook her head, wishing she could blame her depressing thoughts on her pregnancy. "Thanks, but I've had enough."

Jenny recapped the ice cream cartons and tucked them into the freezer. "Okay, then. I'll be out on the patio if you need me."

After Jenny left, Garrick scooted his chair closer and took one of Samantha's hands in his, stroking her skin with the pad of his thumb. "I'm sorry you're not feeling well."

She shrugged. Her attention shifted from the past to focus completely on the sensitive nerve endings in her hand. The warmth of Garrick's palm and the strength in his curled fingers comforted her, and slowly her worried thoughts subsided.

His thumb stroked back and forth, its slight roughness reminding her of the way he'd stroked her whole body the night before. She watched its rhythmic movements, absorbing the sensations.

Samantha swallowed, shocked by her next thought. She wanted him to pick her up in his arms and carry her off to his bed. Right then, in the middle of the day.

Of its own accord, her hand squeezed his.

He squeezed back, his thumb stilling. "Feel better?"

She flushed. "Yes."

She loved him, and the past really didn't matter.

Whatever Warren had been to her foolish adolescent self, he was nothing to her now. She loved Garrick.

Suddenly she needed to show him. Leaning closer, she gave him a soft kiss. She felt the residual coolness of ice cream on his lips, tasted the sweetness that lingered there.

Garrick's thumb started moving again, sending desire skittering along her nerves. "You have a bad effect on me, Sam."

"I do?"

He pulled her effortlessly onto his lap. "I can't resist you."

"Well, um...you don't have to resist me." She wrapped both arms around his neck. "I'm your wife and I love you."

"Thank goodness," he said, his lips against hers.

They kissed for several minutes, then Garrick groaned. "Let's go upstairs," he growled in the huskiest, sexiest voice she'd ever heard.

She didn't hesitate to accept his invitation.

Afterward, lying in his arms as the last shivery sensations faded from her body, Samantha sighed contentedly.

It didn't matter, she told herself, secure in the strength of their bond. The past didn't matter.

"Almost ready?"

Samantha looked up from her dressing table to see her husband standing in the doorway between their rooms. He wore a flawlessly cut black dinner jacket and looked good enough to eat.

She smiled at him, glad she'd allowed Jenny to talk her into buying the ivory silk gown she wore for the play. "Just two more minutes."

She brushed mascara through her lashes, then glanced up to find Garrick still watching her. His eyes held the same glow of desire they'd held yesterday afternoon, the look that said he wanted her with a passion that wouldn't ever stop.

"You're beautiful," he murmured.

Her hand shook faintly. "And you're distracting me."

He laughed, crossing through her room to the hall. "I'll go pull the car around."

Samantha surveyed her appearance in the mirror one last time. She wore her hair down, but pulled away from her face. Beth had insisted on lending her a pair of beautiful pearl earrings and a matching necklace, and they complemented the gown to perfection. All she needed was a dash of perfume and she'd be ready.

On impulse, she pulled open the drawer of her dressing table and sorted through its contents until she found the large cut-glass flacon. She hadn't touched it since her first day back from the hospital, but maybe it wasn't as bad as she'd thought. She'd been upset that day; that had probably clouded her perceptions. And, she told herself now, the bottle was nearly empty, so she must have worn the scent often.

She raised the stopper to her throat and touched it to her pulse-points.

As she did so, a memory assailed her.

Her first thought was, *not another one*. Since her memory in the entrance hall yesterday, the past had become a specter. Her driving need to reclaim it had vanished.

But Samantha couldn't ignore the images crowding her mind. She saw a man handing her a foil-wrapped box. She and Jenny had just graduated from college; they were at a party in the Randall home. Her stomach had dipped with anticipation as she'd carefully opened the package to reveal the perfume.

It was an expensive gift, especially coming from the brother of her best friend. An intimate gift, considering that he hardly acknowledged her the rare times he was around. She'd raised her eyes from the perfume to meet Warren's gaze, feeling suddenly shy. It had been all she could do to whisper a few words of thanks.

Warren.

Warren had given her the perfume. Had given her this cloying scent that didn't match her at all. And she'd worn it regularly.

Why? Out of good manners? From some sense of obligation to the Randall family for their kindness? Or because her crush on Warren hadn't faded?

Samantha put her fingers to her throat to wipe away the scent, then wished she hadn't. Another memory hit her, this one briefer and more physical.

And utterly horrifying.

She felt Warren's lips against her throat, his kisses on her tender skin. She felt her own response. It wasn't arousal—at least not compared to what she felt with Garrick—but she liked what was happening.

Samantha ran to the bathroom. With a washcloth and soap she scrubbed her neck until all traces of the perfume were gone. She felt dirty, almost violated, and though the soap took away the scent, the memory of Warren's kisses remained.

If only scrubbing could get rid of it, too, she thought. If only she could take herself back in time to a few minutes earlier, to reach for a different bottle of perfume and avoid this unpleasant memory altogether.

Samantha patted her neck with a towel, her eyes closed against the past. That kiss hadn't taken place the night of her graduation party, but years later. Her hair had been up in a smooth chignon—instead of down as it had been on her graduation—and she could remember smelling the perfume on herself.

She forced herself to open her eyes and examine her face in the mirror. She had to accept the truth of her memory, accept the fact that her crush on Warren hadn't faded at all, but had grown stronger over the years.

And that kiss. Warren's hungry lips on her throat, her own acquiescence.

It might, very easily, have happened only recently.

She grabbed the countertop for support, praying her imagination was on the wrong track.

What if Warren...

What if Warren was the father of her baby?

Chapter Ten

It would explain so much.

The fight she'd had with Garrick before the accident.

Her periodic feeling that something wasn't quite right.

So what had happened? Had she tricked Garrick into marriage to avoid being a single parent, and then he'd found out and they'd fought?

But if that was the case, then why would he still care for her? Because he *did*. She knew that. No one could be so tender, so absolutely sweet and sexy, without feeling deeply about her.

Could he care for her if he knew what she'd done, if he knew his dead brother had fathered her baby?

Samantha tried to think clearly. Maybe—maybe all her worrying was for nothing. If Warren had died before she got pregnant, then the issue was moot.

Garrick had said it hadn't been long ago. But what did that mean? A month? A year?

Just then Garrick stuck his head around the corner. "The car's out front, Sam."

She started guiltily, as if he could read her thoughts. "One second," she called. She reached for the simple rose perfume she'd been using daily and put it on, taking a deep breath to steady her nerves.

The scent calmed her, reminded her of all the things she and her husband had shared in the past week.

By the time she joined Garrick in the hallway, she had control of her emotions. He didn't know about her new memories, and she planned to keep it that way until she found out when his brother had died. She couldn't ask him right now, not before their big evening out. Not when he thought they still felt the way they had three minutes ago—and when his answer might change everything.

In the hall he took both of her hands in his. "You're beautiful, Sam. So incredibly beautiful." His gaze dropped from her eyes to her mouth. "Do you have your lipstick with you?"

She nodded. "In my bag."

"Good. You can reapply it in the car." He pressed her gently back against the wall, bracing himself with one hand, cupping her waist possessively with the other as he leaned in for a deep, lingering kiss.

Despite her inner turmoil, the caress affected her strongly. She kissed him back, amazed they had such a connection even when something might be so wrong between them.

Finally Garrick pulled away.

"You're covered in lipstick," she said, breathless.

He fished a handkerchief from his pocket and handed it to her. Dabbing at the lipstick, she felt a burst of tenderness for her husband—and also felt, as she never had before, that their intimacy was impossibly fragile. She didn't know how it could survive whatever she'd done in the past.

As they drove down into the city, she tried to keep the fears from her mind. She knew she shouldn't jump to conclusions. But she couldn't stop imagining her deception, imagining Garrick's discovery of it.

Maybe, she thought, he'd been furious and asked her to move out, but her accident had made him feel guilty. He might have resigned himself to a child who wasn't his, to a wife who'd betrayed him; he might have put aside his bitterness to help her through her recovery.

But who knew what he would do once she was completely herself again?

Samantha arrived at the theater with her lipstick repaired but her thoughts still scattered. She sat through the play in a daze, unable to focus on the events unfolding on the stage. During intermission she felt dazed by the crowd, the confused clamor of so many conversations and so much laughter and joviality. She endured the third act with the same restless discomfort, wanting to get home and talk with her husband, but dreading what she would learn.

Finally the performance ended and Garrick led her out of the theater. Seeming to sense her mood, he gave her hand a gentle squeeze.

They were halfway across the lobby when someone called out his name. An elderly woman approached, greeting them both and congratulating them on their marriage. Clearly she knew the Randalls well.

After chatting another minute, the woman put a kindly hand on Garrick's arm. "I was so sorry to hear about Warren, dear. I'm afraid the news didn't reach me until I got back from Majorca...."

Samantha blinked, hearing no more of the conversation. If people were still learning of Warren's death, then it had to be recent—about as recent as her marriage. And she'd been pregnant well before that.

Her throat constricted as anxiety overwhelmed her.

The woman said goodbye and departed. Samantha stared after her. People streamed past, but she didn't notice.

Suddenly she had to know the truth. She couldn't wait another second. "Garrick," she said, her voice low and urgent, "when did Warren die? How long ago?"

Their eyes locked.

"Hell," he muttered. He pulled her through the crowd to a vacant corner of the lobby. "We need to talk, Sam. We really need to talk." He stopped, as if searching for the right words.

"Was it—was it less than three months ago?"

He looked as if he didn't want to answer. "There

are a lot of things you don't know, Sam. A lot of things you haven't remembered.''

Samantha swallowed. ''Tell me.''

''Not here.'' He put an arm around her shoulders, holding her tightly. ''Come on, let's go. I'll tell you everything when we get home.''

Garrick helped his wife into the car, feeling as if the world were coming to an end. Samantha looked pale and shaken and thoroughly miserable.

Which was just how he felt.

Just how he'd always felt with Samantha, having to stand by and watch her worship a man who didn't deserve it. Knowing she'd never see *him*, see that he was madly in love with her and willing to offer all the things she wanted from Warren. Love, companionship, commitment. A family.

He drove in silence, casting occasional glances at her. Samantha stared out the window, her body stiff.

''It's better if we wait until we're home,'' he said softly.

''Why?''

He tightened his grip on the wheel. ''Because our conversation is probably going to upset us both, and I want to get you home safely.''

''What could possibly be so awful?'' She didn't sound curious. More resigned, as if she already knew the truth.

He drew in his breath. ''It's actually not that awful,'' he said. ''Not really. It's just that we...made mistakes. Mistakes we both knew about before your accident. But it's different now, now that you don't remember.''

Samantha didn't respond, just stared out the window.

In the silence Garrick considered what he could possibly say to make everything all right.

Nothing. She already suspected what had happened. She had to, or she wouldn't have asked when Warren had died. She wouldn't have wanted such a definite answer.

And he couldn't keep it from her. His whole marriage might dissolve in the next half hour.

Damn Warren for being such an unscrupulous cad, he thought, too frustrated to feel guilty for it. Damn him for getting them into this mess by his thoughtless, selfish actions.

And damn *himself* for not seeing it coming. He should have, since he'd been well aware of her crush on his brother.

But he'd been so convinced nothing would ever happen. Most of the time Sam's attraction to Warren hadn't been a big issue in any of their lives, because he'd hardly ever been in Portland.

But he'd been in Portland three months ago. Garrick didn't know what had finally made his brother notice Samantha and decide to make her one of his conquests. An excess of boredom, perhaps? A sudden impulse to sink lower than he ever had before and seduce his sister's best friend?

Garrick clenched his jaw, wishing—as he had so many times—that he'd been able to prevent it. But it hadn't even crossed his mind that Warren and Sam might actually consummate their nonexistent relationship.

Then, a couple weeks after Warren had left, she'd shown up at the house, asking how to get in touch with him. And from her obvious distress, Garrick had guessed what had happened—his bastard of a brother had used her and left her pregnant.

He'd felt sick with disgust at Warren, sick with a twisted kind of jealousy. Sick with guilt because he hadn't looked out for her better. But it hadn't stopped him from seizing the opportunity fate had thrown him. Samantha's pregnancy provided the perfect excuse to shift their relationship to a new level.

By then she knew Warren would never take responsibility for the baby. But if *he* did, if he married her and pretended the child was his, they could make a life together. And she might eventually realize the friendship they'd shared for ten years was a lot more like love than anything she'd ever felt for Warren.

They'd married in a civil ceremony. Jenny had been so thrilled that her favorite brother's wish had come true that she'd cried all through the wedding. Samantha had cried too, but not for the same reason.

Garrick pulled his thoughts from the past to negotiate the trickiest section of the road, using all his concentration as he entered the very same stretch of curves where he knew Samantha's car had crashed. As he had each time he'd driven this part of the road, he couldn't keep from thinking about her fragile, unconscious body tangled in the wreckage of her car.

He'd come so close to losing her.

And it was about to happen again. He couldn't stop the truth from coming out.

A minute later he passed through the iron gates and swept up the drive, coming to a halt right in front of the house. Lights shone out onto the sculpted front gardens, illuminating Samantha's strained face.

Garrick got out and circled the car, wondering exactly how much she knew. Wondering if she'd had any memories she hadn't told him about, if that was how she knew about Warren.

By the time he reached her door she'd already gotten out. He helped her up to the portico.

She paused on the top step, as if she'd changed her mind about going inside. "Garrick..."

He gave her arm a gentle squeeze. "Let's go inside."

"Wait. Just tell me something first." She drew herself up, straightening her shoulders. "When did Warren die?"

Garrick felt as though he were stepping off a cliff. "A week before we got married," he admitted.

"After I was already pregnant." It wasn't a question. She stood there for a long time, staring up at the house and visibly struggling with her emotions.

"Sam," he said softly. "Sam. I know what you're thinking."

She met his gaze without blinking. "And I'm right, aren't I?"

He took both of her hands, holding them tightly. "Listen to me, Sam—"

"I'm right."

He gave a defeated sigh, looking down into her beautiful brown eyes. "Yes," he said, "you're right. Warren was the father of your baby."

Samantha stared at her husband, trying to absorb what he'd told her.

Warren was the father of your baby.

Even though she'd been imagining it all evening, the confirmation came as a shock to her system.

She wanted to get back in the car and drive away, to pretend she didn't know anything. She didn't want to get her memory back, not anymore. She wanted to return to the time when she hadn't even known Warren existed, to when she'd been falling in love with her husband and there hadn't been any complications.

Her hands fisted at her sides. "How could you hide it from me?" It came out more accusatory than she'd intended. But she felt so betrayed!

By fate in general, and by Garrick in particular.

He opened his mouth but she cut him off. "No, don't answer that. I don't want to know." She took a deep breath. "I just can't believe it. Did you think I'd never figure it out?"

"No, Sam. Not at all."

This was so awful, she thought. They stood squared off like adversaries, but she couldn't seem to stem her angry words. "You—you manipulated me."

He flinched. "I didn't want to upset you."

"You treated me like a child!"

"Samantha, I'm sorry."

She put a hand to her temple. Her head throbbed.

She thought of Warren's death, of the quick sequence of events. "Did he know?" she asked. "Did Warren know about the baby?"

Silence. Then, "No." His tone held a wealth of meaning, but she couldn't decipher it.

"Why not? There was time, wasn't there?"

"Yes, there was time."

"But I didn't tell him?"

"No."

"How come?" She didn't know why she cared, or why this issue felt so earthshakingly important.

"Because we decided to raise the child as if it were ours. No one needed to know."

"Not even Warren? He was the *father*."

Garrick's expression hardened. "He'd abandoned you. It wasn't any of his business."

She swallowed. "So no one else knows?"

"Jenny guessed. And I think Beth and Hugh did, too." He laughed bitterly. "They all knew I'd never have gotten you pregnant without marrying you first. It had to be Warren."

She didn't know what to say to that. Didn't know quite what it meant. Reaching for the door, she let herself in and started across the front hall. "I should have told him right away. It might have made a difference."

Garrick stopped in his tracks a few feet behind her. "What did you say?"

Her mouth seemed to speak of its own accord. "It might have made a difference—might even have saved his life!" She spun around to glare at her husband. "If he'd known, then maybe he wouldn't have been so reckless."

Garrick's face had gone pale. "Sam..."

Suddenly feeling claustrophobic, she struggled out of her wrap.

He reached out to lift it off her shoulders, his fingers brushing her skin. "Sweetheart..."

She froze.

She recognized the endearment and the tone of his voice. What was more, she recognized the whole situation. It had happened before, one week ago. Right before her accident. She and Garrick had gone out to dinner, and they'd come home arguing over Warren and the baby. She'd said the same things she'd said tonight. Then she'd let him take her wrap, and his hands had brushed her shoulders, just as they'd done right now.

She remembered it so clearly.

And, she realized with a shock, she remembered everything else, too.

Everything.

Chapter Eleven

Garrick watched her, his expression shuttered. "You've had a memory, haven't you?"

Samantha shook her head, looking at her husband with new vision. "No. Not just a memory."

"What, then?"

"All my memories."

Garrick closed his eyes as if the news was painful. "Really?"

Samantha didn't answer. She stood there in the front hall of the Randall family home, remembering every detail of her twenty-five years of life.

Garrick opened his eyes again. Her husband, whom she'd married in a judge's chambers during their lunch hour.

"Are you all right?" he asked.

She didn't answer for a long moment. "No, I'm

not all right,'' she said. The cascade of memories through her brain made it difficult to think clearly. But she knew she was upset.

Because she really had thought she loved Warren all those years. Warren, who'd possessed an outrageous charisma that won over almost everyone.

She remembered how he'd always stolen the limelight from Garrick, despite the fact that *Garrick* was the only one with any substance, the only one doing anything worthwhile with his life. Even their father, she knew, had ignored Warren's irresponsible lifestyle. He'd seen only the dazzling, golden-boy image on the outside.

And she'd been taken in, too. Maybe she wouldn't have been so affected if she'd met Warren a few years earlier, or a few years later, once she'd had more experience with men. But she'd met him at a vulnerable time. She'd fallen for him that first afternoon, and she'd stayed fallen.

With all his glamorous jet-setting, Warren had been around the house just enough for her to see him as an unattainable, mysterious older man, but not quite enough for her to see the real man underneath.

She'd been stupid and naive. And now she felt even more stupid.

Garrick had tricked her. He'd concealed her past from her this past week, pretending the baby was his, pretending they'd married because sexual desire had trapped them with a child. And none of it made any sense.

''We need to talk,'' she told him.

"I know." His voice was gentle and comforting.

All at once she felt like crying. "Everything's wrong," she mumbled. "Nothing's like I thought it was." She felt embarrassed and exposed. She'd told him countless times this week that she loved him, but he'd never said the same thing back.

Garrick drew her into his arms, there in the front hall with the door still open. She slumped against him because she really did love him, taking what comfort she could even though she was upset with him. She remembered what he'd said to her in the hospital: *Love isn't always the most important thing, Sam... Sometimes friendship can be enough.* And now she knew he'd said those same words before, the day they'd agreed to get married.

She'd told him the plan was crazy, that she didn't love him, that they didn't love each other. And he had sat there and told her a marriage based on friendship could be strong enough.

But she didn't know anymore. Was it strong enough? Was it strong enough that she could forgive him for hiding the truth from her? Could she ever forgive him for letting her fall in love with him?

She was vulnerable now, open to being hurt. After Warren's callous treatment, she'd sworn she wouldn't fall in love again. Being in love was dangerous. It had made her do stupid things, had blinded her to Warren's real nature.

She never would have accepted Garrick's offer of marriage if she'd thought love had anything to do with it. She'd married him so her child would have a stable home, so it wouldn't have to grow up with just one parent, without any other family.

Garrick was a safe man to have as a husband. He was a close friend, but nothing more. They understood each other, and there wasn't any danger they would fall in love.

Or so she'd told herself.

What had happened?

Slowly she became aware of Garrick easing her out of his arms. She stood numbly watching as he closed the front door and set her wrap and his keys on the hall table. Returning to her side, he guided her to the family room.

Samantha's eyes wavered as they crossed to the couch. Her gaze fell on the nearly finished jigsaw puzzle and then on the framed photo she'd found the other night.

The photo of Warren.

She turned her back and sat down as revulsion swept through her. She wondered how she'd ever found the man attractive. He and Garrick might have shared similar features and the same dark good looks, but Garrick was the more handsome. At least, she could see that now. Obviously she'd been awed by Warren's flashy charm.

She skimmed her memory, focusing on the various stages of her crush until she reached the night, three months ago, when Warren had pressured her into sex. He'd told her he'd always loved her, that they'd be together forever. Like a silly, lovesick fool she'd thought he meant to marry her, but once he'd gotten what he wanted, he'd left without looking back.

Most ironic of all, their time together hadn't been the culmination of all her dreams. Warren had been an inconsiderate, unimaginative lover. She'd suspected it at the time, and now that she could compare him to Garrick, she knew it with total certainty.

And she also knew the feelings she'd harbored for Warren had disappeared when he'd taken her virginity so selfishly.

She'd tried to tell that all to Garrick. She'd tried...

"But you didn't believe it," she murmured.

Garrick sat on the couch next to her. "Didn't believe what?" he asked.

"Didn't believe I was over him. The night of the accident I tried to tell you." That was what had made her so mad, made her drive off in her car.

Samantha remembered how guilty she'd felt when they'd learned of Warren's death. She'd regretted her decision not to tell him, but she hadn't broached the subject to Garrick until that night a week ago.

She hadn't understood his response. He'd gotten so angry and resentful. They'd argued back and forth before he'd finally asked her how she could still be in love with Warren after all he'd done.

"You thought I wished he hadn't died because I still wanted to be with him," she said, amazed. By then all she'd felt was compassion for Warren. Certainly nothing romantic. "Why, Garrick? What were you thinking?"

He ran a hand through his hair. "I don't know, Sam."

But she didn't need his answer, she realized. All his life, Garrick had witnessed people's fascination with his brother. Their blind adoration of him no matter how badly he behaved. It was Garrick's Achilles' heel—the one thing that clouded his judgment.

"You should have known me better than that," she said. "I might have had a ten-year crush, but once he—" She broke off as Jenny stuck her head through the doorway.

"Hi, guys," she said. "Hugh and I are making brownies. Didn't hear you come in, but then we heard voices. Do you want some? They're almost..." She trailed off and looked from one to the other of them.

"Hello, Jenny," Garrick said.

She smiled weakly. "Oh, hi. You guys are having a private moment, right?"

"Well, yes," Garrick answered. "Actually, Samantha just got her memory back—"

Jenny gave a yelp of surprise. "You did?"

Samantha nodded and watched the play of emotions on her friend's face. Excitement and sheepish trepidation.

True to form, excitement won out.

Jenny bounded over and hugged her. "Oh, Sam. I'm so glad you're okay!"

Samantha thought of how Jenny had acted when she'd first come home with amnesia—she'd been up to her ears in mischief. Samantha gave her a chastening look. "You're in a lot of trouble, girl."

Jenny grimaced. "I know. I know. You can drag me through hot coals anytime you want, okay? But you still love Garrick, right?"

Before she could answer, Garrick said, "We're working on that." He got up and led her to the door. "Go have a brownie."

"They're not ready yet."

"Go, Jenny."

"All right. I'm going." But she stopped in the doorway. "Don't worry, Sam. It'll all work out. Garrick will look after you, just like he promised at the wedding." She disappeared down the hall.

Samantha latched on to her friend's parting statement. Garrick would look after her.

Yes, she thought, he was good at that. Too good. Was that why he'd allowed her to fall in love with him, because he thought it would make her feel better?

It made a crazy kind of sense. It would have been difficult for her to come home from the hospital and be told her marriage was a loveless arrangement, one they'd entered into for the sake of some other man's baby. Even if that was the truth.

It was all out of pity, she realized. Garrick hadn't had the heart to tell her the truth. He'd coddled her.

And the sex part was easy enough to explain. Physical desire, plain and simple. Even if in the past she'd never acknowledged her attraction to Garrick, he *was* an attractive man. Very attractive, though it had taken her a decade to notice.

All his talk about not being able to resist her had

been laying it on a bit thick, of course, but he probably hadn't had much trouble performing. Men were like that, weren't they? They didn't need to be in love to make love. All they needed was an urge. And if there was a little pity thrown in there, so much the better.

God, but she was mad at him.

How on earth were they going to go back to their previous arrangement? She couldn't pretend she hadn't fallen in love with him. Before her amnesia they'd been good friends who planned to raise a small, accidental family. Now were they going to be good friends who slept together?

"I don't want you to look after me," she blurted out. She wanted him to love her back.

Garrick stood in the middle of the room, looking exhausted. His dinner jacket was all rumpled from holding her.

"Look," she said, getting up from the couch. "I need some time to think." She walked past him, all the way to the front hall. She needed to be alone, she realized, to come to grips with how the past few days had affected her life.

"Sam, wait."

She turned to face him, not caring what she said. "Why? So you can give me more pity? I don't want to be coddled. I'm having your dead brother's baby! You tricked me into loving you! You hated Warren and you're going to hate his child!"

Before Garrick could speak, she grabbed his keys off the table and darted outside, slamming the heavy door closed behind her. She ran to his car and slipped behind the wheel, locking the doors before he got there.

She would drive somewhere quiet—maybe to her old apartment or to a hotel—and think things through. She had to know what to do next.

Garrick pounded on the windows. "Sam, come on," he said. "Come back inside."

She rolled down the window a crack, just enough so she could talk without yelling, but not enough so he could get his hand in and unlock the door. "Garrick, I need some space."

"Fine. Just don't take it in a car. Or don't you remember what happened the last time you drove away from here?"

She remembered. She'd been confused, hurt and crying. She hadn't been able to see the road, and she'd been driving too fast. A sickening feeling filled her as she remembered the moment she'd known the car was skidding out of control. She'd seen the tree coming toward her, known she was going to hit it, known she was probably going to die. And all she'd been able to think about was getting back to Garrick. Getting back to Garrick so she could tell him she'd just realized she loved him.

Oh, God. She *had* loved him before her accident. Tears misted her eyes, and suddenly racking sobs overtook her body as she struggled to come to grips with this knowledge. She slumped against the wheel, letting the confusion wash over her.

Slowly her mind cleared and she saw it all laid out

in front of her. She'd been falling in love with him for years. Their friendship had grown and developed into something else, but she'd never noticed. She thought back to the water fight with Garrick, knowing all sides of it now. She hadn't thought about that moment in years, until she'd remembered it during her amnesia, and she'd never, ever, interpreted her feelings as desire for Garrick. She'd blamed those odd sensations on wishing Garrick had been Warren. Obviously a distant, unreachable crush had seemed preferable to a mixed-up relationship with her second-best friend.

Garrick had his fingers through the window of the car, as if he could touch her if he just tried hard enough. "Sam, open the door. Please."

She reached blindly for the lock button and flipped it up. Garrick swept the door open and lifted her out of the car, holding her against his chest. "It's okay, Sam. Everything's okay."

She sniffled, hating feeling out of control. "Put me down, please."

He did, but he still held her against him. "Are you okay, Sam? I'm worried about you. And about the baby."

"Warren's baby," she muttered.

"Your baby," he corrected, his voice firm. "*Our* baby."

"Okay then. The baby and I are both fine." She paused, swallowing. "Why didn't you tell me?"

He was silent for a long time before answering. "I

wanted you to have a clean slate. I wanted you to fall in love with me.''

''You *wanted* me to fall in love with you?''

''Yes.''

''You weren't just...just being nice out of pity?''

Garrick shook his head emphatically. ''No, Sam. Pity is the last thing I feel for you. I want to have a real marriage. That's what I've always wanted.''

Her heart hammered. She could barely breathe. ''What do you mean, always?''

''From the first time I saw you.''

She remembered back to that moment. For some reason the idea of it annoyed her. They'd wasted so much time. ''Garrick, I was fifteen!''

''I'm well aware of that. It was the exact opposite of what you thought in the hospital. It always has been. I've been madly in love with you the whole time, but you never saw me as anything but a friend.''

''So...so is that why you married me?''

He nodded. ''Don't get me wrong, Sam. I wanted to give your child a safe home and two loving parents, just like I told you. But I also hoped that living with me, sharing the responsibility of raising a child, would make you slowly fall in love with me. I was prepared to wait years. But when you woke up in the hospital and thought we were already in love, I couldn't bring myself to contradict you. I took a shortcut, and I'm sorry.''

''But—but it was true, Garrick. We *were* already in love.'' She told him about the moment right before her crash, how she'd realized she loved him as her car spun off the road.

His arms tightened around her. "Oh, Sam, if I'd lost you..."

"I think that's why our fight upset me so much. I had all these escalating feelings for you, and all you could talk about were my supposed feelings for Warren."

"I'm sorry. I was just so jealous, and our marriage had made me possessive. I was a real bear that night."

"It's okay, Garrick. I love you. And as long as you love me, too, I think I could forgive almost anything."

He kissed her forehead. "Should we go reassure Jenny and Hugh that everything's okay?"

"Only if we can go straight upstairs afterward. I want to be alone with you."

"Deal."

"Do you think they know the crazy way we fell in love?"

Garrick nodded. "I think they do. You know, it was obvious to everyone but you that I was madly in love with you, and it wasn't that hard to tell you had a thing for Warren, either."

Samantha sighed. "I made a fool of myself over him, didn't I?"

He didn't answer.

"Admit it, Garrick."

"A little," he said, a grin lighting his face. "But it brought us together, didn't it?" He placed a warm hand on her stomach. "And it gave us a precious gift to start our life together."

She looked up at him, feeling suddenly vulnerable at the mention of Warren's paternity. "You don't mind, really?"

He shook his head. "I love this child more than I thought possible. Because he or she comes from you, and because this child is what finally brought us together. It doesn't matter who the father is—we'll make him or her completely ours."

She couldn't keep from grinning. "I love you, Garrick."

"And I love you, too, Sam."

Epilogue

Samantha turned sideways, examining her silhouette in the mirror. She laughed at what she saw. Her lacy white wedding gown flowed down over the less-than-subtle swell of her abdomen. "You don't think it's too ridiculous?"

"You look lovely, Sam. Doesn't she, Mom?"

"I look like a pregnant lady," Samantha countered. "And pregnant ladies don't wear wedding dresses like this. But I should just give up on getting an impartial opinion from the two of you." She allowed Beth to pin her veil to her hair. "We really should have done this a while ago, before I started to show quite so much."

"Big weddings take time to plan, Sam," Jenny told her, not for the first time.

"I know. But I think this is going to end up embarrassing Garrick. Our picture in the paper is going to look pretty silly.''

Jenny turned to her mother. ''I think she's nervous.''

''Nervous? I'm not nervous! For goodness sakes, I'm only marrying my own husband.''

Beth and Jenny exchanged a look. ''She's nervous,'' Jenny said.

Beth gave her shoulder a squeeze. ''It's okay, Sam. I know how important this is to you. The last time you married Garrick, it wasn't because you loved him. Now you do, and that's a big difference. Marrying for love is always a bigger deal.''

Samantha gave her mother-in-law a wry look. ''Okay, so I'm nervous. All I can say is, Garrick had better not laugh at me as I come down the aisle.''

Beth stepped back and surveyed her with a judicious eye. ''I don't think there's much danger of that, my dear. No danger at all.''

Jenny smiled. ''We'll be lucky if he doesn't take one look at you, call off the ceremony and take you away to ravish you! You look gorgeous. Pregnancy becomes you.''

''Speaking of calling off the ceremony,'' Beth commented with a wink, ''we'd better get moving so he doesn't think you've changed your mind.''

Entering the crowded church a few minutes later to the strains of the wedding march, Samantha had eyes only for her husband. He stood at the altar, looking resplendent in a dark gray morning suit, and even from her distance she could see the love and desire shining out of his eyes. He was smiling, but with happiness, not amusement, as she came belly-first down the aisle.

Samantha knew, looking at him, that they shared a love that would last their whole lifetimes, no matter what else happened. She quickened her steps toward him, eager to pledge her love.

*   *   *   *   *

**This summer, the legend
continues in Jacobsville**

Diana Palmer

A LONG, TALL
TEXAN SUMMER

Three **BRAND-NEW** short stories

This summer, Silhouette brings readers a special
collection for Diana Palmer's LONG, TALL TEXANS
fans. Diana has rounded up three **BRAND-NEW**
stories of love Texas-style, all set in Jacobsville,
Texas. Featuring the men you've grown to love from
this wonderful town, this collection is a must-have
for all fans!

*They grow 'em tall in the saddle in Texas—and
they've got love and marriage on their minds!*

Don't miss this collection of original Long, Tall Texans
stories...available in June at your favorite retail outlet.

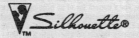

MILLION DOLLAR SWEEPSTAKES
OFFICIAL RULES
NO PURCHASE NECESSARY TO ENTER

1. To enter, follow the directions published. Method of entry may vary. For eligibility, entries must be received no later than March 31, 1998. No liability is assumed for printing errors, lost, late, non-delivered or misdirected entries.

   To determine winners, the sweepstakes numbers assigned to submitted entries will be compared against a list of randomly, preselected prize winning numbers. In the event all prizes are not claimed via the return of prize winning numbers, random drawings will be held from among all other entries received to award unclaimed prizes.

2. Prize winners will be determined no later than June 30, 1998. Selection of winning numbers and random drawings are under the supervision of D. L. Blair, Inc., an independent judging organization whose decisions are final. Limit: one prize to a family or organization. No substitution will be made for any prize, except as offered. Taxes and duties on all prizes are the sole responsibility of winners. Winners will be notified by mail. Odds of winning are determined by the number of eligible entries distributed and received.

3. Sweepstakes open to residents of the U.S. (except Puerto Rico), Canada and Europe who are 18 years of age or older, except employees and immediate family members of Torstar Corp., D. L. Blair, Inc., their affiliates, subsidiaries, and all other agencies, entities, and persons connected with the use, marketing or conduct of this sweepstakes. All applicable laws and regulations apply. Sweepstakes offer void wherever prohibited by law. Any litigation within the province of Quebec respecting the conduct and awarding of a prize in this sweepstakes must be submitted to the Régie des alcools, des courses et des jeux. In order to win a prize, residents of Canada will be required to correctly answer a time-limited arithmetical skill-testing question to be administered by mail.

4. Winners of major prizes (Grand through Fourth) will be obligated to sign and return an Affidavit of Eligibility and Release of Liability within 30 days of notification. In the event of non-compliance within this time period or if a prize is returned as undeliverable, D. L. Blair, Inc. may at its sole discretion, award that prize to an alternate winner. By acceptance of their prize, winners consent to use of their names, photographs or other likeness for purposes of advertising, trade and promotion on behalf of Torstar Corp., its affiliates and subsidiaries, without further compensation unless prohibited by law. Torstar Corp. and D. L. Blair, Inc., their affiliates and subsidiaries are not responsible for errors in printing of sweepstakes and prize winning numbers. In the event a duplication of a prize winning number occurs, a random drawing will be held from among all entries received with that prize winning number to award that prize.

5. This sweepstakes is presented by Torstar Corp., its subsidiaries and affiliates in conjunction with book, merchandise and/or product offerings. The number of prizes to be awarded and their value are as follows: Grand Prize — $1,000,000 (payable at $33,333.33 a year for 30 years); First Prize — $50,000; Second Prize — $10,000; Third Prize — $5,000; 3 Fourth Prizes — $1,000 each; 10 Fifth Prizes — $250 each; 1,000 Sixth Prizes — $10 each. Values of all prizes are in U.S. currency. Prizes in each level will be presented in different creative executions, including various currencies, vehicles, merchandise and travel. Any presentation of a prize level in a currency other than U.S. currency represents an approximate equivalent to the U.S. currency prize for that level, at that time. Prize winners will have the opportunity of selecting any prize offered for that level; however, the actual non U.S. currency equivalent prize if offered and selected, shall be awarded at the exchange rate existing at 3:00 P.M. New York time on March 31, 1998. A travel prize option, if offered and selected by winner, must be completed within 12 months of selection and is subject to: traveling companion(s) completing and returning of a Release of Liability prior to travel; and hotel and flight accommodations availability. For a current list of all prize options offered within prize levels, send a self-addressed, stamped envelope (WA residents need not affix postage) to: MILLION DOLLAR SWEEPSTAKES Prize Options, P.O. Box 4456, Blair, NE 68009-4456, USA.

6. For a list of prize winners (available after July 31, 1998) send a separate, stamped, self-addressed envelope to: MILLION DOLLAR SWEEPSTAKES Winners, P.O. Box 4459, Blair, NE 68009-4459, USA.

SWP-FEB97

**AVAILABLE THIS
MONTH FROM
SILHOUETTE
ROMANCE®**

And the Winner Is...
You!

...when you pick up these great titles
from our new promotion at your
favorite retail outlet this June!

Diana Palmer
The Case of the Mesmerizing Boss

Betty Neels
The Convenient Wife

Annette Broadrick
Irresistible

Emma Darcy
A Wedding to Remember

Rachel Lee
Lost Warriors

Marie Ferrarella
Father Goose

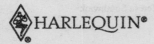 

As seen on TV!
Free Gift Offer

With a Free Gift proof-of-purchase from any Silhouette® book,
you can receive a beautiful cubic zirconia pendant.

This gorgeous marquise-shaped stone is a genuine cubic
zirconia—accented by an 18" gold tone necklace.
(Approximate retail value $19.95)

Send for yours today...
compliments of ▼ *Silhouette*®
™

To receive your free gift, a cubic zirconia pendant, send us one original proof-of-purchase, photocopies not accepted, from the back of any Silhouette Romance™, Silhouette Desire®, Silhouette Special Edition®, Silhouette Intimate Moments® or Silhouette Yours Truly™ title available in February, March and April at your favorite retail outlet, together with the Free Gift Certificate, plus a check or money order for $1.65 U.S./$2.15 CAN. (do not send cash) to cover postage and handling, payable to Silhouette Free Gift Offer. We will send you the specified gift. Allow 6 to 8 weeks for delivery. Offer good until April 30, 1997 or while quantities last. Offer valid in the U.S. and Canada only.

Free Gift Certificate

Name: _____

Address: _____

City: _____ State/Province: _____ Zip/Postal Code: _____

Mail this certificate, one proof-of-purchase and a check or money order for postage and handling to: SILHOUETTE FREE GIFT OFFER 1997. In the U.S.: 3010 Walden Avenue, P.O. Box 9077, Buffalo NY 14269-9077. In Canada: P.O. Box 613, Fort Erie, Ontario L2Z 5X3.

FREE GIFT OFFER
084-KFD

ONE PROOF-OF-PURCHASE

To collect your fabulous FREE GIFT, a cubic zirconia pendant, you must include this original proof-of-purchase for each gift with the properly completed Free Gift Certificate.

084-KFD

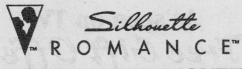

Silhouette
™ R O M A N C E ™
COMING NEXT MONTH

It's a month of your favorite wedding themes! Don't miss:

#1234 AND BABY MAKES SIX—Pamela Dalton

Fabulous Fathers/It's A Girl!
Single father Devlin Hamilton agreed to a *platonic* marriage with lovely Abby O'Reilly. Their children needed a real family—and Devlin and Abby could help each other without the added risk of true love. Until a surprisingly passionate wedding night led to a new family addition!

#1235 THREE KIDS AND A COWBOY—Natalie Patrick

Second Chance At Marriage
Playing the part of the loving wife wasn't difficult for Miranda Sykes. She still loved her soon-to-be ex-husband, and Brodie needed her to adopt the orphans he'd taken in. But Miranda hadn't realized that three kids and a cowboy just might change her mind about staying around forever!

#1236 JUST SAY I DO—Lauryn Chandler

Substitute Groom
A fake engagement to dashing Adam Garrett would finally rid once-jilted bride Annabelle of everyone's pity. But when sparks started to fly between her and her substitute groom, their arrangement didn't feel like a game anymore! Could Annabelle get Adam to just say "I do" for real?

#1237 THE BEWILDERED WIFE—Vivian Leiber

The Bride Has Amnesia!
Dean Radcliffe's nanny had lost her memory...and thought she was Dean's wife and mother of his children! Until Susan remembered the truth, the handsome single father had to play along, but could it be this bewildered woman was meant to *truly* be his wife?

#1238 HAVE HONEYMOON, NEED HUSBAND—Robin Wells

Runaway Bride
After jilting her two-timing fiancé, Josie Randall decided to go on her dude ranch honeymoon—alone. Falling for wrangler Luke O'Dell was the last thing she'd expected—but the brooding, stubborn rancher soon lassoed her love, and had her hoping this honeymoon could land Luke as a husband!

#1239 A GROOM FOR MAGGIE—Elizabeth Harbison

Green Card Marriage
A marriage of convenience to her arrogant boss was drastic, but Maggie Weller would do anything to stay with Alex Harrison—and care for his adorable little girl. But Maggie's green-card wedding led not only to a permanent position in Alex's home, but to a most *unexpected* place in his heart!